A SHA

MW01206411

THE
DEAD OF
WINTER

Diane M. McPhee

BLUE FORGE PRESS

Port Orchard ✸ Washington

The Dead of Winter
Copyright 2024
by Diane M. McPhee

First eBook Edition May 2024
First Print Edition May 2024

ISBN 979-8-89439-001-7

For information about film, reprint or other subsidiary rights, contact: blueforgegroup@gmail.com

Blue Forge Press is the print division of the volunteer-run, federal 501(c)3 nonprofit, Blue Legacy (EIN 83-4307421), founded in 1989 and dedicated to supporting artisans marginalized due to race, age, disability, economics or other factors. We strive to empower storytellers from all walks of life with our four divisions: Blue Forge Press, Blue Forge Films, Blue Forge Gaming, and Blue Forge Sound. Find out more at www.BlueForgeGroup.org

Blue Forge Press
7419 Ebbert Drive Southeast
Port Orchard, Washington 98367
blueforgepress@gmail.com
360-550-2071 ph.txt

For all those who are homeless; the state of having no home or permanent place of residence.

> *The why's and the wherefore's don't matter*
> *Only the voice and the plea*
> *For a stranger to stop and to care*
> *About people that no one can see*
> *—Art*

ACKNOWLEDGMENTS

While writing this book, I rented a small office in the downtown area of a neighboring town. From my second-floor window, I would occasionally look out and watch people as they hurried into the restaurant across the street or walked to the few stores on the block. It was a military town and I enjoyed seeing men and women in uniform, usually with visiting family, also walking by.

Sometimes, from my writing desk, I noticed a disheveled man or woman pushing a loaded shopping cart or toting several bags as they slowly ambled down the street. A couple of times I heard screaming and looked out to see a man losing control and hitting at parked cars while shouting and swearing to no one in sight. One time, as I was unpacking things from my car, a young man came up behind me and asked for money. I was startled but reached into my bag and pulled out a couple of dollars. He thanked me and walked away. It was later that I thought how differently this encounter might have resulted, and I admit I became more cautious. But I also got into the habit of carrying an extra water bottle to hand to someone sitting in a doorway or I would stop to greet a person who seemed to have lost their way.

Learning about homelessness has been an education. I read books, watched movies, scoured the internet, and thought about the people in my own life who live without shelter. It happens. My characters are fictional, but their circumstances are seen in every city across the nation. I hope my readers will be able to understand and appreciate a little more about life on the street... especially, the loneliness.

I am deeply grateful to my dear friends who read and helped edit my book. Your support and timely suggestions have been instrumental in making this book a reality. And my heartfelt thanks to Blue Forge Press for encouraging me to write another Alan Sharp mystery. Your belief in my work has been a constant source of inspiration.

THE
DEAD OF
WINTER

Diane M. McPhee

FRIDAY, JANUARY 24TH

Winter in Boston. Dark in the morning and dark on the commute home. Moderate to heavy snow was in the late January forecast and would most likely impact the late day travel. Streets were already icy and cold, and people were bundled against the chill of the wind that whipped around and through them, lowering the air to below freezing. Luckily, the subways were running on time. A homeless man stumbled onto the downtown train and settled into a seat by the window. His weather-beaten face and musty clothes annoyed the commuters, but he appeared unconcerned. He rode the subway as far as he could on days like this to unclench his hands against the biting cold wind and dry his soaked shoes. The lights flickered as the car slowed to a stop, and the man glanced out the window and saw a body lying motionless at the end of the platform. Without thinking, he jumped up and waited anxiously for the door to open, and then he pushed through and sprinted down the tunnel to help.

The scene was gruesome. The body of a man was slumped on the concrete floor, bloodied, and beaten with strangulation marks around his neck. The homeless man took his pulse in case he was still alive. He was dead. Afraid that someone would think he's involved, he yelled to alert anyone exiting the cars, but no one was paying any attention to the scene. He searched the pockets for the victim's ID and found a police badge. He was a cop!

Waves of confusion caused the man to panic and fear that he would be blamed for this murder. Charging up the steps to State Street from the subway exit, he ran into a crowd of commuters who were battling the weather. He began to walk briskly... hoping to make the traffic light... trying not to fall on the slippery street and bring attention to himself. But then he remembered the strangled face on the person he left behind and he started shouting at everyone to get out of his way. He weaved through the crowd, changing speed, cutting left and right to avoid groups of people, forcing himself to focus, trying not to panic. He dodged and then tried to bulldoze his way through, shouting the whole time. He held tight to his backpack full of all his belongings, which was coming loose from his shoulders.

The bedraggled man became addled and stumbled into the nearest open door, shouting, "Officer down! Detective down!" and collapsed onto the floor.

MONDAY, JANUARY 20TH
FOUR DAYS EARLIER

W hat did you just say?" Detective Alan Sharp stopped in front of a young officer and looked him square in the eyes. In fact, he had to look up because the officer was at least three inches taller than Alan's 5'11".

The officer turned around and was surprised to see the senior Detective staring at him. Automatically saluting out of respect, he took a short breath and repeated what he had just said, "I believe that most homeless people are homeless by choice, sir." He blinked several times and waited for the possible and likely reprimand.

"Explain yourself," Alan said, glancing at the officer's badge. New recruits had recently been assigned to the busy Boston downtown precinct. His name was Wagner.

Officer Wagner shifted from one foot to the other. "Well, sir, I think people who are homeless should make better choices. We should stop making excuses for them... stop them from blaming their personal problems on broader economic and social forces."

Alan stepped back to continue the conversation. "Are you referring to the low-income housing and incentive programs offered by the city? Are you saying that homeless people shouldn't be allowed to take advantage of those?"

Feeling frustrated with the attention he was causing, Wagner tried again to explain his point of view. "All I'm saying is that these programs might give them a secure roof over their heads, but it doesn't require them to get sober or get treatment for mental illness."

Alan wasn't certain if this was a challenge, or if the younger man truly believed that the chaos on the street could be easily solved. Over the years, he had advised his officers that there were two sides to one story, and then there was the truth. "Do you understand that homelessness is a traumatizing experience? And that people with addictions and mental illness are more likely to improve when they have access to housing?"

Officer Wagner nodded and cleared his throat. "Sir, I understand this. But these programs don't require homeless people to get the help they need. And in the meantime, there's the pressure we're getting from citizens who complain about needles in the park and shopping carts rattling on quiet streets. They want us to remove encampments and institutionalize or arrest anyone homeless who uses drugs, abuses alcohol, or begs on the streets."

Several thoughts flashed through Alan's mind. "I suppose you feel the same way about food being handed out each day." Alan was trying to hold his temper, thinking that the younger generation didn't begin to understand the problems that society faced.

Officer Wagner was not going to give up. He shifted his weight back and forth and then continued, "Anytime you give out services without treatment I believe that's enabling. As much as I appreciate the hot meals for free, food isn't helping folks on the streets. It may help them today... but not tomorrow. You've got to serve food in a place where mental health service is being provided. Sir."

Alan sharpened his focus on the young officer. "How do you think people who are homeless survive without food and what little help they do get? What do you suggest? Imprisonment? And what else would be a good antidote? Let me tell you my friend, the general public has done a pretty good job of desensitizing themselves and mastering the art of not seeing people sleeping in doorways."

Perhaps second-guessing his decision to speak out, Wagner relented. "Yes, sir. You're right. What do you want us to do?" The officer looked around the room, hoping to find support from the silent team of officers. But no one moved.

Alan addressed the group. "We'll do something. We need to learn how to be more sensitive and understanding with a new approach. Within the week, I hope to be handing out the first steps of a plan."

Alan shook his head and wondered if taking on this part-time administrative job for the district was going to work. The Deputy Superintendent had called him into his office last week and asked him to step in as temporary captain for five to six weeks while Captain Murray, his friend and colleague, was on medical leave. This position meant not only working with his own investigative detectives, but Alan would now be supervising patrol officers, including young officers just out of the academy. Alan expected all new recruits to understand that their job was to exercise good judgment and make quick decisions to de-escalate conflicts, but he wondered if Officer Wagner understood those responsibilities.

Alan walked into his office and tossed his gloves on to

the cluttered desk. January had already broken weather records for low temperatures, and snow was predicted again this week, which meant icy streets and traffic jams. How did people on the street manage in such cold weather? Sitting down on his squeaky swivel chair, Alan thought about the many people who had lost their homes. He knew that the combination of low wages and rising house rents led many workers to wind up sleeping in their cars, on friend's couches, on the street or in shelters. In no state, metropolitan area, or county can a worker earning federal or local minimum wage afford a modest two-bedroom rental home by working a standard 40-hour week. To make it worse, landlords often evicted lower-income renters who then wound up on the streets or in overcrowded quarters.

Alan picked up the phone and called his friend Carla.

Carla Tompkins was the director of the Teen Center in the Back Bay. Her program was designed to help troubled and at-risk teens transition their lives in positive directions. When Alan called, she had been enjoying a conversation with his son, Sam Sharp, her employee for the past year. Sam had been hired to do research but was eventually promoted to counseling teen clients who knew him from the intramural basketball team he had organized. She was impressed with this young man and knew everyone who worked with him felt the same way. Carla had to smile to herself, because she believed Sam was more like his father than he wanted to admit.

Alan had called to discuss the homeless program she had tried to fund over a year ago. Her co-worker, Marko Miller, had been the driving force behind the project, but had been brutally murdered during an arson in the Back Bay. Her desire to continue the program was set aside while she grieved the loss of her friend. Maybe now was the time to review the homeless program and do something positive in memory of Marko. She called Sidney.

Sidney Miller was between clients at his busy law office in Government Square. When he saw his phone light up and noticed it was Carla, he smiled. "Hello pretty lady!"

Carla just loved this man. He was Marko's older brother, and it was the unfortunate circumstances of losing his brother when they met. Sidney now volunteered at the Teen Center and offered advice to those who needed legal help. He never thought he did enough, but Carla always praised him for all he did.

"Good morning, I have a quick question... do you remember the homeless program I told you about that Marko was working on? I think I want to review it and get it up and running. Can you help me with this?"

"Of course. Send me the proposal he was working on, and I'll see what we need to do to get it started. Is there a special reason to work on this now?"

"Alan called me this morning and wanted to get advice about starting an incentive program for his officers dealing with the homeless. I guess there are some very conservative attitudes hanging around the precinct that need some changing. Alan wants his officers to become more aware of the conditions and reasons for homelessness. I like this idea... educating the department with a little empathy."

"Leave it to Alan to want to make a change. I'll give him a call later and see what's up." Sidney and Alan had also met during Marko's investigation and had formed a friendship.

They were both in their mid-sixties and found they had a lot in common. It was Alan who pointed out their differences... Sidney was an elegant Black lawyer who carried himself with dignity, while Alan considered himself an untidy working cop who resembled that detective on TV who had OCD. What was that guy's name?

Sidney made a note to call Alan and meet him for a drink. It had been a while since they met up and checked in with each other.

Detective Enrique Mendez knocked on Alan's office door and quickly entered. "What's up for today?"

Alan made a motion for Enrique to close the door and then pointed to a chair. "I'd like your views on something that's bothering me. What do you think about the new recruits we have in the patrol unit?"

Enrique was surprised that his superior officer even thought twice about the younger officers. "What do you mean? Their experience? Their reports?"

Alan looked out at the squad room. Every officer appeared to be busy or preparing for their shift. "How did you decide to become a policeman?"

Raising his eyebrows and smiling slightly, Enrique shook his head. "What's this about, Alan? My background is different from a lot of these new recruits. You know I grew up in a rural area in Belize... responsibilities were clear, and self-discipline was necessary. We had a work ethic that included personal relationships... you know, interacting with people... not by computer or phone. I'm not that old, but I feel ancient when I deal with all the social media and programming that's out there now."

Alan nodded. "We both learned decent problem-solving skills... and our parents didn't rescue us from every predicament we got into. I'm worried that a few of the new recruits don't have the maturity or life skills and street smarts to make good decisions. I'm wondering if they even know how to de-escalate a potentially dangerous situation. Is it their age or their lack of maturity?"

Enrique smirked. "Age and maturity don't always go side by side... I know a 45-year-old who acts like a child. But I know what you mean... we seem to be correcting the younger officers for not addressing their superiors by rank, and fielding questions from them on why they can't have assignments like ten-year veterans. There seems to be a lack of motivation."

"I just had a talk with Officer Wagner about the homeless situation. He seems to be stuck in his views about the city not doing enough, which although I agree, his attitude is conservative enough to get him into some trouble. I want him to ride with you for a couple of days and tell me what you think."

Enrique hesitated. He hadn't been on patrol for some time and since he was a detective, he felt it was a step down for him. "Can't you get one of the senior officers to step in?"

Alan explained further. "I'm meeting with Carla Tompkins later today to see if we can come up with a plan to become more aware of the homeless problems. We have feet on the ground and it's about time we assist and not just arrest. I want you to talk with the organizers and volunteers at the shelters about the work they're doing. These people probably learn more about the lives and experiences of people on the street and have a better understanding of the complexities of homelessness. Having Wagner tag along may give him a better idea of the crisis many people face."

"I'll ask Marie for her help, too. She knows a few nurses who volunteer at the clinics for homeless clients. I think they might be another good resource." Marie and Enrique had been married for twelve years and were raising three daughters. She was a part-time nurse at an elementary school and kept up with the news around the hospitals and clinics. Enrique knew she'd be happy to help.

"Make your phone calls and then let Wagner know he'll be riding with you. I want you to determine his attitude and approach to the situations on the street and let me know how it goes." Alan smiled at his friend. They had been through a lot over the years, and he was glad to have Enrique back after months recuperating from being shot during a hostage situation. It could have been much worse, and both men knew they had been very fortunate. Enrique had recovered over the holidays and the doctor said he was ready to be assigned. But Alan still wanted to ease him back into the busy police precinct.

Enrique knew Officer Gary Wagner already had a reputation. He had heard some older officers complain that Wagner was irresponsible and a little arrogant, lacking emotional intelligence and street sense. This seemed harsh to Enrique, and he hoped they were overstating their views. Looking around the squad room, he spotted Wagner sitting and staring at his computer. When Enrique walked past him, he noticed social profiles dash across the screen. "Officer Wagner? Are you busy?"

Wagner quickly closed the screen down and jumped to attention. He hoped the Detective hadn't noticed the profiles of women he was screening. "No, sir. I'm not busy."

Enrique wondered if Wagner was on a dating site. He had learned about these sites because of the last case he and Alan were involved in. A young girl and an older woman had been caught up in social media sites that had put them in great danger. The woman had been killed, but the girl survived. Remembering this, Enrique stared down at Wagner. "I've got a few phone calls to make and then I want to talk to you about an assignment."

Officer Gary Wagner automatically wondered if his argument with Detective Sharp had gotten him in trouble. Gary had never been one to mince words. Growing up in a house with three older sisters, he had no choice but to hold his own and learn to argue convincingly. He used this determination on the basketball court, too, when he made the varsity High School team as a junior. He was fast and tall enough to play a scoring guard position and lucky to have a great coach who made him work and reminded him that the game was seventy percent mental and thirty percent skill. As a result, Gary developed an unwavering desire to win. Confidence in himself and his high school team led them to win the playoffs two years in a row.

Gary was a week away from his twenty-ninth birthday. His sisters chided him for not being married yet, but he liked single life. Sometimes his oldest sister accused him of being a control freak because of his need to micromanage everything in his life. But he didn't consider himself compulsive, he just liked the security of avoiding any surprises and doing things his way. He rented a one-bedroom apartment in the Back Bay district and was content to master the routines he set for himself. To him, that was well-grounded independence.

Gary watched Officer Mendez walk away and hoped he

hadn't been caught on Tinder. Lately, he worried he might be addicted to viewing all the profiles of potential dates on this site. Apparently, he was a good catch because his profile received several "likes" by the hour. He never thought of himself as handsome by regular standards, he was tall... that helped... but he hated that he was losing his hair. He used to have thick blond hair, but now wore a crew cut. His sisters thought his green eyes were his best feature and teased him that girls would be attracted to them. But he thought wearing the police uniform in a couple photos gave him as many points as he needed to impress possible dates.

That evening, Enrique was pleased when Marie came up with a list of volunteers to interview at the homeless shelters. He was surprised to see the familiar young deacon's name on the list when Marie handed it to him. "Are you certain Deacon Martin volunteers at the shelter?"

"Positive! And everyone loves him. He's so young and full of energy. He also has great insights on how to get more support from donors. He brings a fresh approach to the group with his ideas."

Enrique was skeptical. "From my experience, younger people don't always sign up to volunteer for very long and also have shorter attention spans, not to mention their love of technology."

Marie knew her husband had old-fashioned ideas and rules about behavior. "Well, they're more likely to help do physical chores and activities. And when was the last time you did an excel program?" A smile flitted across her face. She then felt embarrassed for bringing Enrique's limited mobility into the discussion. His months of physical therapy from being shot had left him weakened, even though he kept faithful to the exercises. She quickly added, "I wish I had more time to volunteer. I'm sure they need all the medical help they can get."

Enrique agreed. "I'll let you know what I find out."

It was cold and damp and Alex warmed himself by the smoldering fire beside his tent. Inside his tent were bags of clothes and pots and pans, along with a dirty rug, and soaking shoes. He was worried because he learned the city was about to evict everyone at the camp because of safety concerns. They said it was because of allegations of rape and prostitution, but the homeless knew it was about complaints of public-health issues... piles of garbage, heaps of personal possessions and rats. So many rats. They scurried wildly across the mud and under the pallets that separated the tents from the ground.

Alex had adopted a life in a homeless community two years earlier. He lived without running water, safe heating, or any way out. "It's crippling," he told anyone who will listen, "and not only are people sleeping in tents, in doorways, in green spaces, on beaches, in cars, trucks, RVs... the list can go on... but so many of us have figured out how to live this way long-term." He took out a ragged frying pan and started to heat up a can of Spam. He wondered if it would snow.

TUESDAY, JANUARY 21TH

Officer Connie Beale watched Gary Wagner talk to Detective Mendez with interest. Was he going to get an extra assignment because of his outburst yesterday? It would serve him right because she was tired of his nasty attitudes. She had ridden with him several times and then requested to be reassigned due to scheduling problems. But the real reason was because of his ranting about people he thought were a lower caste than his privileged self.

Connie was one of five women officers in the busy precinct and was often frustrated by the lack of female support. She knew that one reason women were reluctant to apply was because of the inflexible schedules police work required. Assignments often required overnights, and even holidays and birthdays which were sacrifices, especially for working mothers. Connie met one policewoman who had to use her vacation time to attend her child's school events, including conferences. Knowing of the struggles women faced, Connie volunteered for extra assignments to help the women with children who needed more flexibility. She knew that Detective Sharp listened to the complaints of scheduling, but he didn't offer any solutions. He told them he would like to hire more women to better reflect the community but there had to be changes in recruiting strategies and even advertising. That meant providing women with necessary resources which included mentoring and leadership training. All of this cost money that the taxpayers refused to support.

Connie had two rules she used as a foundation for being a police officer. Number one was respect and the other was voice. When she was on duty she responded professionally and gave everyone an opportunity to comply. She believed that a person's humanity was the last thing they possessed, and she never wanted to take that away. And no matter how many domestic calls she had to listen to, she responded to each voice with fairness, even if it was a violent, screaming person.

Connie knew there was a big difference between how men and women officers responded to calls… men tended to act aggressively. That was why she couldn't ride with Gary Wagner. He would respond emotionally and sometimes with anger if a suspect pushed his buttons. Whereas Connie used her brain to respond, he relied on his physical strength to get people to comply.

She now watched as Wagner turned away from Detective Mendez with a perturbed look on his face. She noticed how he hastily grabbed the equipment from his desk and slapped on his jacket. It looked like he was going on an assignment with the Detective, and Wagner obviously hadn't expected that.

"What's up?" Connie asked Wagner as he passed by her.

"Nothing… just going out." He didn't even look at her.

Something was wrong. Searching the room to find out who would know, Connie saw Sasha Lane enter the precinct. She was a role model for Connie, and they often shared confidential concerns about their jobs, hoping for guidance and sometimes instrumental support. "Hey, Sasha... do you know what's going on with Wagner?"

Sasha kept her voice quiet as she revealed what she knew. "I guess he's being assigned to patrol the homeless camp areas. It's probably because of what happened yesterday... you know Detective Sharp would never let that outburst go without addressing it again."

Both women appreciated DS Sharp and respected the decisions he made, especially when teaching a lesson to someone who may have stepped over the line. He did this not only to have them dig deeper into their own truth, but it was also a safety issue. And for Alan, this far outweighed the lesson.

Alan pulled up Officer Wagner's profile on his computer to find more information about his background. He read that Wagner grew up in a small town in South Carolina and had three siblings; he went to school locally and then on to USC where he played basketball on a scholarship. When he graduated, he played on some international teams and then at twenty-seven entered the police academy. No criminal records or misdemeanors, so it looked like he was either lucky or followed the rules. Why did Alan feel there was something missing? He decided to call his friend at the academy and see if he knew anything about Wagner.

"Alan! What's the occasion? When was the last time we spoke to each other?" Simon Garrison was delighted to hear from his old friend. They had known each other since academy days but rarely got in touch since they graduated and went on with their lives.

"Simon... it's good to hear your voice. I don't often get

to D.C., but if I did, I would look you up. Right now, I've got a question about one of my recruits. Gary Wagner was in the academy last year and has ended up in my precinct. What can you tell me about him?"

Alan could hear Simon typing on his computer. "Okay... let's see... it looks like he was smart... second in his class. He was an okay cadet... had a basketball reputation and, in fact, played a lot on breaks. I know he was competitive... liked to win... but that's not anything new because most of these guys and gals are pretty aggressive."

"Any problems? Complaints?"

"Well, Alan, this is interesting in a funny kind of way. He seemed to like to eavesdrop."

"What do you mean? Listen to conversations secretively? Why would he do this?"

"Yeah, he was caught lurking around listening and would often repeat what he overheard. It was immature. I guess people complained. Some of the cadets felt they couldn't discuss anything private around him because they felt betrayed in a way."

"Was he ever disciplined?"

"No, as far as I understood. It reminded me of a guy I knew... a smart student who graduated first in his Princeton Law class and became a popular lawyer. For the most part, he was a great guy, but he had this one flaw... or a hobby as he called it... he eavesdropped. He said it was good entertainment and taught him a lot about people and human communication." Simon gave a small chuckle.

Alan didn't agree. "Hmm... it seems to me that justifying eavesdropping would, by extension, justify other offenses like cheating, being a peeping tom, shoplifting, or even having an affair. I hate the idea because there's always a victim."

"Well, Alan, we're of a generation with a different moral compass. What else can I do for you?"

"If that's all you have on him then I'll let you go. When are you going to get up my way, Simon?"

"I'll let you know." The two friends rang off.

Alan put Wagner's profile in a folder and looked at the time. Carla had asked him to join her at a town meeting and he only had fifteen minutes to get there. The meeting's agenda included a homeless task force organization that hoped to build mutual support and combine efforts and resources with different groups around the city. They were going to discuss a standardized set of goals, processes, and strategies. If Alan was serious about implementing change in the precinct, this would be a good place to network with people who wanted change, also.

Carla met Alan at the door and rushed him to a seat. The first speaker was the one she wanted him to be sure to hear. Carla believed this man was going to stir things up.

The speaker appeared young, although it was difficult to gauge because of his bald head and well-trimmed beard. Alan watched him and was impressed with the energy he exhibited when he walked on to the stage. He held his shoulders straight and stood to his full six feet and then leaned courteously to listen to the shorter woman who would introduce him to the crowded room. They laughed at something that was said, and then both peered out into the boisterous audience. The man nodded his head and then stepped back, as the woman approached the microphone and waited for the noise to die down.

"Thank you for your attendance today. Many of you know our speaker, Nick Grainger, who has been mentioned in several articles and in many circles for his generous altruistic acts for the homeless. I know some of you don't like the word 'homeless' and prefer to say 'displaced.' Nick acknowledges both, along with 'rough sleepers,' and appreciates your understanding. Today he wants to tell you more about the urgent need for volunteers to help implement a coordinated outreach plan to help move people off the street and into shelters. Please welcome Nick with me."

The room filled with applause as Nick stepped to the microphone. In a low, yet passionate voice, he began. "Let me tell you what I have learned about social volunteering from people on the street... rough sleepers... the homeless. Their greatest desire is not a hot meal, clean clothes, or a roof over their heads. This may surprise you. What they truly desire is for someone to share their life with. A companion, a friend. They are lonely." Nick took a minute to look at the crowd. He wondered how many felt the same need in their busy lives.

"This makes displaced, lonely people not 'the other' but more like us. They have met life at its worst and maybe should be seen as valued and resilient. Perhaps even considered as our neighbors. As a volunteer, you could bring goodwill by the simple act of sharing conversations, anecdotes, and other ways of being human. Just like you treat your friends and families."

Again, Nick let that sink in. The room remained still. Nick continued. "When, and if, you become a skilled social volunteer, you will be trained with rights and responsibilities. You will be trained well. We send you out as ambassadors who will be able to assess the needs of people who live without homes and help advocate for them. You will learn how to respond to a crisis and make a judgment that guarantees the rights of everyone involved through mediation. You will help to share in our vision to make people's lives better."

Nick took a moment to look around the room. He spoke a while longer about how people can support the programs that are set up around the city. His final words were important. "So many of our neighbors are left to suffer and languish on the streets. I think about the freezing weather we are experiencing now. Several of you will be asked to volunteer at night and sometimes the weather will be below freezing and there will be a lack of adequate care for people you meet. Don't worry. We are equipped to supply blankets, tents, and sleeping bags... whatever is needed... because it's our collective responsibility to act. These basic acts of kindness we extend to people on the street will always be appreciated." He left the stage, hearing murmurs of approval.

Carla looked at Alan, hoping for a reaction. He was nodding and writing in his notebook. "I'd like Mr. Grainger to come and talk with my officers and explain this to them. I sometimes think we've lost the humanity in our approach to the ongoing program of relief. I like everything he said."

"Nick works tirelessly on this approach. I'll text his information to you. The remaining speakers are concerned with rescue theories that are more long range... permanent housing, counseling, health care, job training... you know the drill. You can stay and listen if you want."

Alan agreed to stay and take notes.

WEDNESDAY, JANUARY 22ND

Enrique looked around the squad room and then signaled for Officer Wagner to follow him. Settling at his desk, Enrique directed Wagner to have a seat while he pulled up a list of people. "Yesterday we drove around to make a list of the camps and shelters surrounding the city. Today, Detective Sharp wants us to interview volunteers at the shelters to see firsthand what they need from us." Enrique looked up to see Wagner's response. Seeing none, he continued, "At this point, our presence has mixed response. Some people like and agree with police procedures and others want us out of the picture."

Wagner nodded, keeping his opinions to himself. "I'm ready to go, sir."

Enrique was pleased with the show of respect from the officer. He quickly grabbed his heavy jacket to ward off the cold weather that had reached the low twenties overnight. It concerned him that people were surviving out on the street without appropriate clothing or shelter. They would see what was needed, and report back.

The downtown shelter was tucked back on Pine Street, a tall brick tower that was once a fire station lookout. It appeared to be a sturdy and reliable building that was capable of withstanding the harshest weather. Like most growing cities, it was surrounded by wealthy condos and apartments that seemed in contrast to the need that was seen on the street.

Deacon Levi Martin met the two officers at the entrance. "It's good to see you, Mr. Mendez... or I mean Officer... or is it Detective? Sorry... how's your wife?"

Enrique was amused with the younger man. He must be in his mid-twenties and still had the look of a teenager. His long hair was pulled back into a ponytail that hung down his back, and his Indian heritage was apparent in his facial features. He was as tall as Enrique, and when he shook hands, his grasp was firm.

"My wife is fine, thank you. Officer Wagner and I would like to have a look around the shelter and see what help we can offer. Are you free to give us a walk through?"

"I'm free, but first I have to visit the encampment down the street to make sure they have the supplies they need to combat this weather." He grabbed some blankets and looked at the officers. "Would you mind walking with me?"

"Of course," Enrique quickly said, "what can we carry?"

Loaded up with more blankets and food supplies, the three men walked the several blocks to the encampment. Enrique had often been called to this homeless group to break up fights, and he knew it was largely recognizable from a distance by trash, assorted containers, cardboard, and abandoned tents. To the naked eye, not much ever changed in most encampments, and they would find buckets of human waste along with the trash. Being homeless did not bring out the best in people.

As the three men walked the littered path, they noticed

two of the four tents in one group were toppled over and abandoned. Levi pointed to one unoccupied disheveled tent, "It belongs to an old guy who's been arrested for threatening a city official with a weapon." The officers peered inside and saw cans of food, three backpacks, several pairs of old shoes and mounds of clothes.

"It looks like he has quite a lot of stuff," Officer Wagner said, showing some amount of disgust.

Levi nodded. "That's the thing... people regularly drop off items at the camps. Everything from food, clothes, appliances, water... these are all left in a pile at the entrance. Each day people from the camp sift through the articles and claim what they need, or what they consider they might need in the future."

"So, they just hoard things?" Wagner seemed annoyed.

"Well, they might be able to sell what they're given and feel they're progressing in some way. We know that most people are struggling to get out of this situation, but some are seasoned homeless who consider this the only way of life."

Enrique looked at Wagner's perceived annoyance and wondered about his background. He might have grown up with privileges, or without, but his negative attitude seemed to give rise to some prejudice that might get him into trouble.

After distributing blankets and supplies, the three men walked back to the shelter. People were already lined up outside for the noon meal which wouldn't be served for two hours. Many of them were huddled close together to keep warm and nodded at the officers as they passed. Levi greeted many of them, using their first names. As they entered the shelter, Levi said, "I wish we could open the doors all day, but we found that the disruption of just a few would sometimes frighten our volunteers who were busy in the kitchen."

Enrique looked over at the several ladies who appeared to be enjoying their time together. "Are those regular volunteers?"

"Two of them are regulars. The lady with the red glasses and the one next to her are best friends. Corinne and Lola... they come every day to fix and serve lunch. It's their kitchen if you know what I mean?" Levi gave a slight smile and then waved at the kitchen crew.

The shelter held three dorms, one for men, another for women and the third for teens. Each dorm had bunk beds that were neatly made up with blankets and pillows. "Who makes the beds?" Enrique asked.

"The people who stay the night make their own beds. Once they're accepted into the dorm, they have the bed for ninety days. But if you're late getting here, you lose thirty days. And if you don't comply with the other rules, you're out. Keeping your space neat and clean is important."

"What are the rules?" Enrique asked.

Levi hesitated to answer. There were several rules and regulations that were kind of a tool kit to cover all the responsibilities a person had when staying at the shelter. "Basically, rules involve curfew, no phones or Walkman's, mandatory medication, no drug, or alcohol use. We have counselors available to offer support. There's just a lot going on... "

Enrique understood. The homeless crisis always had medical and psychological issues that needed to be addressed along with the basic needs of shelter and food. "I know that some people on the street are often found in doorways, park benches, alleys, under bridges and even ATM alcoves... not in the shelters. Do you think some people prefer the outdoors rather than a bed here?"

Levi smirked. "Detective, have you ever tried to sleep in a shelter with a hundred other people in the same room?"

Enrique grimaced. "No... I see your point."

Officer Wagner finally spoke up. "But I've heard there are apartments people can sign up for... for free... "

Levi looked at the officer with curiosity. "That's true... but there are long waiting lists and some of those apartments are plagued with rats hanging around garbage cans, and broken windows, cement floors, conditional plumbing... and the city thinks that's good enough." He shook his head, as if picturing the filthy places he had seen.

The men continued to look around the shelter. There were eighty bunk beds in each dorm, which would never be enough for the hundreds of people who needed shelter. Levi continued to comment. "We hope the city will keep the South station open for a kind of informal wintertime shelter. The mayor has made a deal with the owner during the winter months to let the homeless stay there after midnight." Levi glanced sadly at the people lined up at the door. "We're talking about human beings here."

The shelter felt cold today, but Trevor had no choice but to stay because it was freezing outside. With the wind factor, it had to be in the mid-twenties by now. Twice he had slipped on the black ice because he couldn't distinguish the cold winter sheen from the bare concrete. When he stepped into the doorway of the noisy crowded room, the guard stopped to twirl the wand over his body, searching for weapons. He didn't have a weapon on him. Sometimes he wished he did, but he knew that might get him killed if it got into the wrong hands.

The smell of the noontime meal drifted over the tables as he made his way to the back of the line. There were hand wipes to use, and he would need more than a couple because of the mess he made crawling through the dumpster on Mass Ave. He thought he had seen a newer car drive up and throw a bag in the trash and he wanted to see if there was anything worth having or selling in the contents. He was in luck... he had found a half pack of cigarettes in one bag. This was like gold. He buried the cigarettes deep in his backpack and would be able to trade them for necessities, like medication and warm clothes. He wished he had something to drink right now to warm him.

Looking at the lunch offering, he saw they were serving mini turkey meatballs on rolls. The strong smell of garlic reminded him of home.

"What are you thinking?" The voice from the other side of the counter came from the church lady who usually served meals on Wednesdays. She had a comical look on her face, and he didn't know what to say.

"Huh?"

"I saw you zoning out for a minute and wondered what you were thinking about. I don't mean to pry, you just looked thoughtful." The woman then seemed to dismiss the conversation and moved things along to the salad bar. Speaking louder than necessary, and sliding his tray along, Trevor blurted out, "I was remembering when my mother always put garlic on tuna."

Beside him, another person spoke up, "So did my mom...

36

in case the tuna was on the old side. There's nothing like the taste of garlic to hide the smell of garbage."

When the officers returned to the precinct, Alan asked to talk with Enrique without the younger officer present. "How did it go?"

Enrique took a chair beside Alan's desk and hesitated. "Do you want to know what I think about Wagner, or about the shelter?"

"Both... start with the shelter." Alan listened intently and wished he had more resources to focus on the homeless proposal he was hoping to get started. But he had a busy precinct to oversee and would have to find time to work this into his agenda. He finally asked Enrique's opinion about Officer Wagner. "Besides his views on the homeless, do you get the sense that he's holding on to some prejudice about the way things are run around here, too? He appears to have some superior notions, and I'm wondering if it includes this department."

Enrique thought for a minute. "He definitely has a problem empathizing with people on the street and might have a disadvantage or distrust with officers who show compassion. Maybe it's time to put him on patrol with someone who has a better understanding of the complexities of what people deal with to survive on the street."

"Any suggestions?" Alan knew Enrique had better communication with the patrol officers.

"I like Officer Lane. She has a way of focusing on vulnerability and resilience and is well respected."

Alan nodded. "Good idea. Have Officer Lane come to see me when she's free? In the meantime, Enrique, let's consider what our team can do for the homeless. Can you get some ideas going? Why don't you call Carla and see if she's free to come in and speak to our precinct. She's planning to start a program we may be able to help her with."

Enrique agreed, and immediately called Carla for help.

THURSDAY, JANUARY 23RD

C arla liked the idea of speaking with the department and arrived at the precinct early to talk with Alan and Enrique. She appreciated being asked to speak but didn't want to appear to have all the answers. "Maybe today I'll give a few examples of how desperate the situation has become along with suggestions on how to better accept and interact with people on the street. What do you think?"

Alan smiled at his long-time friend and trusted that whatever she said would be noteworthy. "This is our first approach to opening a discussion about this subject. So, anything you want to say will help our ongoing plan of action."

The precinct officers were instructed to arrive at 8:00 for the monthly in-service training meeting. Most of them held large containers of coffee and blinked at the speaker as if to wake up for the first time. Alan introduced Carla and then let her take over.

"Good morning. My name is Carla Tompkins and I'm pleased to recognize a few of the officers in this precinct, and always happy to see women officers present." At this point Carla nodded to the five women in uniform. "I've been asked to speak this morning about the homeless population. To begin with, there are generally four categories: One—people who might be hiding in a rented storage locker; two—those who are briefly homeless; three—the ones you find on the street a few times a year, and then four—the 'chronic' who are the rough sleepers in tents, alleyways, doorways, or those in shelters. We all see them, people who are in crisis... some are lone figures in apparent stupors wandering around, yelling at cars, stoned jaywalkers... or folks shooting up in doorways... men and women asking for help... and so you wonder... what can you do?" Carla looked around the room as if she had asked for an answer.

"One thing you can do is accept them. Learn to listen and allow people to tell you what's going on with their lives. Let them know you have compassion and that you care because it's important for street people to know the police well enough to trust them. You can start by knowing the name of the person you meet and addressing them by their surnames. Treat them as you would your neighbors. Show them the respect they fear they've lost forever." Carla looked around the room and then added, "Of course, there's a need for diplomacy and to use some restraint... but learn not to push too far." Carla paused for a moment. "Sometimes I think we've lost our purpose and love for each other. Maybe it's competition that has blinded our compassion and maybe anger that caused this separateness. You might be conflicted, confused, or unsure on what steps to take, but remember that *you* are free to make decisions, *you're* in control of your own lives. Homeless folks have lost all that."

Carla then spoke about reasons people lose their homes and dignity. "A stunning number of people on the street are well-educated and highly skilled. Many hold jobs or receive financial aid, but they still can't save enough money for rent.

Anyone can wind up homeless with just a stroke of misfortune. And so, any figment of normalcy you can offer is welcome. A little generosity and humanity can go a long way."

As Carla spoke to the officers, Wagner heaved a sigh. He was working through all the possible scenarios he had witnessed on the street, every emotionally tense situation, and he knew things were seldom as they appeared. To him, the city was falling apart and becoming more unsafe due to the politics surrounding low level criminal activity which included the homeless. He still believed that many of the street people chose to stay homeless because of addictions. And addicts won't or can't quit, and dealers would never quit selling to them. It disgusted Wagner to know that if dealers ever got caught, they counted on and were given minimal consequences. It was all part of the system.

Alan was watching Wagner while Carla talked. Obviously, the officer's mind had drifted, and he looked bored. He then glanced over to see Officer Sasha Lane taking notes. He knew she was serious about her job and so he looked forward to speaking with her after the meeting. He looked up to see Carla staring at him with concern.

"Detective Sharp? Is there anything else I can say to help your program?"

Alan felt embarrassed to think she caught him not paying attention. "Thank you, Carla. I hope everyone has something to take away with them as they go about their day. We plan on having weekly meetings about reaching out to people in a more positive and caring way." Looking at the group, he dismissed them.

Carla walked over to Alan with a slight smile on her face. "Was I interrupting something?"

Alan shook his head. "No, not at all. I was watching one of my officers to see how he was reacting to what you were saying. I have a meeting with another officer right now, but maybe we can get together later to discuss a plan of action with Enrique. I want him to handle this program."

They decided to meet at Carla's Teen Center at 4:30.

Officer Lane was waiting for Alan at his office door. Sasha was a 35-year-old Black woman who was raising three children as a single mom. She managed her job and home life because of help from her mother who cared for the kids and sometimes stayed over when Sasha had to work nights. Alan knew that Sasha was studying for the detective exams, and he had all the confidence in the world that she would become a first-rate detective.

Once again, Alan was struck by the serious nature of this experienced officer as he offered her a chair. He watched as she took out her notebook and pen, preparing to listen intently. "Officer Lane, thank you for your time. I have an assignment for you. I want you to ride along with Officer Wagner as a training assignment and monitor his behavior over the next few weeks." Alan watched as Sasha's eyebrows raised and a look of wariness crossed her face.

Alan continued. "He's had some cautions filed against him for the use of excessive force in the past two months. As you know, this always makes it difficult and even dangerous for the whole department because we get repercussions from the public."

Sasha nodded but still appeared uncertain. "Sir, what exactly do you want me to do? Correct him?"

"No, the bottom line is that his behavior and style of interactions with citizens needs to change. I want you to report back to me any actions that go against the guidelines each officer is expected to follow. I need Wagner to develop a better range of responses for maintaining authority without abusing the public. I'm asking you to be his role model for a brief time." Alan let that sink in and watched as the officer thought this through.

"So, let me see if I understand... do you want me to coach him or watch him?" Sasha wanted clear guidelines as to what approach she was to take.

Alan didn't expect her to become a street-corner psychologist or have the proper skills to help someone overcome hostility, or defensiveness. He continued to explain. "I don't need you to develop solutions, just give me feedback in the form of reflective views so I can begin to understand the broader reasons for his negative behavior. You don't need to push. My focus will be on correcting the problem behavior, not bashing him. And, of course, this will stay confidential."

Sasha nodded. "When do I start?"

"Tomorrow. Today I want you to ride with your regular partner. I'll make new assignments and post them by morning. Several officers will be reassigned, so it won't look like you have been singled out."

Sasha stepped outside of Alan's office and stopped to review the job she had been assigned. She had far less involvement with her fellow officers because of her busy family life, and now she was going to be riding with one who had the reputation for being contemptuous. She reminded herself what her mother would say... 'If you don't know, you don't judge.' Sasha would try and keep an open mind.

Gary Wagner didn't appreciate being assigned to desk duty after spending yesterday following Detective Mendez around the shelters. He had hated seeing the filth and rot that people lived alongside, and he was more surprised to see that the white population in the camps outnumbered the people of color. He was even astonished to see so many women. To him it was all a sickening reality. Why would anyone choose to live like that? Today he had been assigned to contact public health, housing, welfare, education, and legal systems to find out what new policies have been enacted. At least that kept him in the warm squad room instead of out on the windy streets.

Alan and Enrique arrived on time to meet with Carla at her office, even though the weather had dipped into the low twenties and the streets were icy. On Thursdays, her busy center was open to homeless teens offering food and an evening clinic, and young people were already lined up to meet with doctors and nurses who offered treatment and meds. Alan noticed a table filled with jackets, socks, and blankets labeled free. Carla thought of everything.

She met the officers as they waded through the crowd. "Let's go to a conference room in the back." The room was comfortable and appeared to be a staff lounge. Carla offered coffee but the officers declined. They sat at a table and started asking questions.

"What kind of treatment do you offer the kids?" Enrique was surprised by the number already there.

Carla dropped her chin to her chest and shook her head. "I wish we could do more. These kids are drug addicted, some are suicidal, most have childhood trauma but what I see is loneliness." She looked up at both officers. "So many of these kids have mental issues and wander alone on the street. It breaks my heart."

Alan could see the tears in the corners of Carla's eyes. "Carla, we want to help. Let's find a way for our police department to be proactive." The meeting lasted for two hours.

The teen was raging down the middle of the street. His filthy jeans were hanging loose and falling off his hips. His hair was wild and seemed to match his anger. He began hitting at parked cars and yelling "Leave me alone! Get out of my way!" People on the sidewalk were using their phones to record the teen who was in obvious danger. Nobody approached him. When he heard the sirens, he ran into a nearby alley. He just had to get to the shelter. Another man chased after him.

FRIDAY, JANUARY 24TH

The Boston weather held steady at two degrees below freezing at what the forecasters called chilly. There were sharp winds off the Charles River and cars on the bridge were passing by a man who sat shivering in his wheelchair. No one could stop to help, but phones lit up at the precinct to report what they saw.

Alan had just walked into the precinct when he heard about the emergency. "I need two teams to go help the guy on the bridge... he's in a wheelchair so I also called the EMT's to see what they can do."

Two officers immediately stood and put on their heavy coats. Alan looked for more volunteers and then pointed to Wagner and Sasha. "I want you both to go."

Sasha glanced at Wagner and then began grabbing supplies. She knew to focus on providing relief of any kind... blankets, gloves, and first aid. Wagner, on the other hand, slowly stood and put on his jacket. He didn't know why he was paired with Officer Lane instead of his regular partner and let out a loud sigh.

Alan watched Wagner's reaction to his new assignment and then strolled through the busy squad room and walked into his office. His office felt cold, like the weather outside. He had other things to worry about today than the young officer.

Reaching into his pockets before taking off his heavy coat, he felt several pieces of paper. Alan had a habit of loading his pockets with notes or receipts and so he decided to take time and throw out what he didn't need. Tossing the several items onto his messy desk, he noticed there was writing on one of the receipts that looked like a message. He picked it up and read, 'Remember: Monday 3:00.'

Alan sat down on his old swivel chair and tried to remember who might have given this to him. He didn't recognize the handwriting and wondered if it was placed secretly in his pocket. He turned over the receipt and read that it was from a hardware store in Watertown. That was miles away. Looking carefully at the amount and purchase, Alan saw that paint brushes and cleaning supplies had been purchased for $45.39. The transaction was cash, and the date was last Friday.

What was he doing last Friday? He knew he wasn't in a hardware store or even close to Watertown. But somebody wanted to give him this message. Who? What did he forget? This would take a while to think through. Once again, he felt frustrated with thoughts of aging and forgetting things. He hated the fact that at sixty-six he was labeled a senior citizen. He didn't feel old, and he knew several people who worked until they were almost eighty! He felt okay health-wise although his back bothered him sometimes. He had even cut down on carbs and now watched his diet. And he walked more. Taking out his calendar, he wrote, Monday, 3:00... question mark.

When Wagner returned to the precinct, he passed the scheduling board and saw he was assigned to ride with Officer

Lane for the next few weeks. He inhaled sharply and looked around to find her. Sasha was writing notes on her computer about the man on the bridge when Wagner approached her.

"What's this about? Why am I riding with you now?" He appeared annoyed.

Sasha decided to try and appeal to his human side. A smile flitted across her face as she spoke, "Guess you're just lucky. I'm going to finish up with this report and then we can get going. We have the North side today."

Wagner stomped back to his desk and began cracking his knuckles. It was an annoying habit he had since he was a teen because he thought it released some tension. And right now, he needed more than relief. Why did he have to team up with this officer? Maybe he did get on the wrong side of Detective Sharp, and this was his punishment.

Connie watched Wagner walk away from Sasha's desk. She saw from the assignments that those two would ride together and she wondered how Sasha felt about it. She decided to find out. "Hey, Sasha, want to get together after work today?"

Sasha looked up at her friend and nodded. "Let me make sure my mother can stay late and I'll let you know. How about 5:30 at that place by the subway on State Street?"

Connie wrote the time and place on her calendar and took off to start her patrol duty. She had a new partner too, so she and Sasha could compare notes when they met up.

Sasha's drive with Wagner proved interesting. Wagner didn't hesitate to quiz her on the department's policing policies. What did she think about the body cameras? Did she think that drones really helped solve crimes? He asked her about high-speed pursuits and even the use of force. When Sasha didn't respond fully to these questions, he finally asked, "What would you say your personal style for policing is, Officer Lane?"

Sasha was driving the car and watching the road, glad that she didn't have to look at her partner. "Do you think we all should have personal styles?"

"Yeah. We were taught different styles at the academy. You know, like the enforcer who protects and believes in strict law enforcement, or the realist who sees problems but with no solution."

"I'm neither. What other styles are there?"

"The optimist... who helps everyone but gets frustrated because social order is so low. And then there's the idealist who believes every person has a good side. So, what are you?"

Sasha thought this was a trap. She had heard that Wagner liked to repeat conversations and mix up the context to make other officers look bad. She would have to be careful. "I don't know what my style is. What's yours?"

Wagner looked out the window and wanted to be careful. He knew he was already in trouble because of his views on the homeless, so he decided to play it safe. "I never thought these categories were very practical. It seems that each department needs all different kinds of styles to operate a fully functional department." He began popping his knuckles in a rhythm that made Sasha believe he wasn't aware he was doing it. *Pop. Pop.*

Sasha was interested. "I agree. Do you think our department is functioning in this way?"

Wagner shook his head. *Pop. Pop.* "Personally, I wish there was more assertive law enforcement. We need to go after serious crimes and stop wasting time on minor violations." *Pop. Pop.*

"Do you mean, use aggressive force?" She probably sounded irritated, but the popping was beginning to annoy her.

"If necessary. I just get tired of those people who become cynical and avoid conflict because they think they can't do anything about crime." *Pop.* Wagner glanced at Sasha, hoping he hadn't gone too far. He finally realized he had been cracking his knuckles and held his hands tightly.

"Well, Officer Wagner, we're always lectured to maintain a certain standard of professionalism. We have procedures to follow that are set up to protect our safety along with the public in general." Sasha let this sink in for a minute and then changed the subject. "Do you want to stop somewhere for coffee?"

The conversation the rest of the day remained civil, yet cautious. Sasha watched Wagner's approach to people who they stopped for minor offenses and noted his frustrations. When they passed several encampments, he seemed to clench his hands and let out deep sighs. She didn't want to press the issue but made a mental note to address this with Detective Sharp.

At 5:30 Connie and Sasha arrived at the restaurant on time and found a table near the window. Both ordered a glass of Pinot. "How was your day with Wagner?" Connie asked.

"Interesting. He asked a lot of questions. He's got some strange ideas about police styles and enforcing the law. I wonder if he was in the military before the academy."

"I heard he was some basketball star. He played in

college, I don't know, maybe even some international leagues, too."

"Well, maybe that's it. He might have witnessed some aggressive law enforcement in other countries that he preferred. Or maybe he's just a physical and competitive guy. He has this annoying habit of cracking his knuckles. It was so irritating! How did your day go?"

The two officers shared a large order of nachos as they reviewed their day and laughed about their personal lives. Connie was younger and dating an officer in another crime unit. "Hey… do you know if Wagner has a girlfriend? Between you and me, I saw him looking at profiles of women one day."

"I have no idea. I don't keep up with anything outside the department. But he did check out early today… maybe he had a date." Both women rolled their eyes. The dating world was beyond them.

Just then the door to the restaurant flew open and a man dressed in a ragged coat and carrying a large backpack came stumbling in yelling, "Officer down! Officer down!" Sasha and Connie immediately jumped up to help. Was a fellow officer in trouble?

Alan had stayed late at the precinct to make a few phone calls and was still trying to remember if he had an appointment on Monday or not. His phone rang just as he was packing up to go home.

"Sir, this is Officer Lane. We have an emergency… Officer Wagner was just found strangled in the State Street subway!"

"Who's with you?"

"Officer Beale is here, and I've called for an ambulance.

We're sealing off the area as best we can and waiting for additional officers. What would you like us to do now?"

"I'll be there shortly. Begin interviewing witnesses."

The scene was gruesome. Officer Wagner's body was found slumped over on the subway floor. He appeared to have been beaten and strangled. Lloyd Randell, the medical examiner, arrived behind Alan and knelt respectfully beside the body. It was Randell's job to establish the cause and time of death. He could already tell it was a violent attack and unnatural death that might involve some amount of criminal activity. He shook his head repeatedly, thinking of how much of a loss this would be for the young man's family and friends.

Alan quickly surveyed the gathering crowd and spotted Officer Lane talking with several people who were either witnesses or curious citizens. Taking out his phone, he quickly took a video of the people who were converging around the crime scene. He needed a record of these onlookers.

Sasha walked over to the Detective and began reviewing what information she had gathered. "The man who ran through the street and into the restaurant is named Vince Robarts. He claims to have found Officer Wagner's body in the tunnel because he was seeking shelter. Apparently, Robarts stays in one of the storage compartments when he can." Sasha looked up from her notes. "I don't know if what he says is true, in fact we had to pry this out of him because, of course, it's against the law to find shelter in the subway tunnel."

Alan quickly asked, "Did he see anyone at the scene?"

"No. He said he was on the subway and looked out on the platform and saw the body. He looked for ID... probably more than that... and saw his badge. That's when he went running. He said he was trying to get help when he ran out of steam and collapsed inside the restaurant."

"Okay, do we have him in custody?"

"Yes. He's at the station. We've interviewed some commuters, but nobody heard anything. Maybe the incident happened earlier. I've taken down the names of people who are here now, but I think they're just curious to see what's going on."

Alan scanned the crowd again and then walked over to talk with Randell. "Lloyd, do you have any indication of the time of death?"

Randell removed his heavy black rimmed glasses and nodded. "I would say it happened within the last two or three hours. You know how wary I am about giving TOD, but this looks recent."

Alan looked at his watch. It was 7:15pm. He would have to find out when Wagner got off work and figure out the time frame for when he met his assailant. But now, someone would need to collect the CCTV surveillance videos from all points of view to find out if anyone was following him. He called Officer Lane over. "Can you get the CCTV footage from the surrounding areas?"

"Yes, sir. I'll ask Officer Beale to help me." Sasha first called her mother and asked her to spend the night. She knew there would be more questions to answer about her earlier drive with Officer Wagner along with details about the people she interviewed. It would be a long night.

Alan's next thought was contacting Gary Wagner's immediate family. The press would be all over this and he wanted them to be protected from hearing it on social media.

After a few phone calls, Alan contacted the sheriff in the small South Carolina town where he learned the Wagner family lived. Police Procedural Manuals wrote up a template to help officers who had to relate the sad news to families, but this time, the local sheriff knew the family personally and said he would take care of it. Sheriff Carroll informed Alan that Gary had three sisters who still resided in the town along with their aging parents, Henry and Helen. He would let them know and make certain they had resources for support.

When Sheriff Carroll showed up with the terrible news, Henry Wagner opened the door. He could tell by the look on the Sheriff's face that it would be something bad. "Come on in, John, and tell me what happened." Wagner led the Sheriff into the den.

"Henry, I've got some terrible news. It's about Gary... he was found dead late today. Apparently, he'd been beaten and, I guess, strangled. I am so sorry." John reached out to pat Henry's shoulder. "Where's Helen?"

Henry couldn't think. Grief seemed to take hold of his whole being and all he could think of was not seeing his youngest child alive ever again. The sheriff saw the emotion overwhelm his friend and quickly stood up to get him some water. He had been to the house many times over the years and knew his way around. When he returned to the den, he saw that Henry had begun to cry. Just then they heard the front door open.

"Henry... what's a police car doing out front?" Helen's voice rang through the house. When she saw John, she stopped and let her purse fall from her hands and spill onto the floor. "John... what happened? Where's Henry?"

John walked over and held Helen's hand as he led her

into the den. Henry didn't even hear them approach as he silently wept. Helen fell to her knees beside him and rocked him back and forth. "Tell me, dear, what is it?"

In tears, Henry related what John had told him. Helen sat back on the floor and caught herself before she completely fell over. "No! That can't be true!"

John helped her get up to a chair and quickly walked to the kitchen to get her a glass of water. He was trying to hold back tears and be of assistance to his friends. The next difficult call would be to their daughters.

Alan heard from Sheriff Carroll late in the evening. He was told that Gary Wagner's family was in shock. The last time they all had been together was over the recent holidays when Gary spent three days with the family and seemed in great spirits. "Personally," the Sheriff remarked, "being the only son, his parents expected a lot from him. He ran with a loud crowd, mostly sports kids, but otherwise kept to himself. He was a good kid, and smart, too. I always thought he would go places because he was ambitious. The whole town is going to be just sick about this."

SATURDAY, JANUARY 25ND

Whenever an officer is killed, the city takes a deep breath. The Police Commissioner and Mayor gave press releases to the media praising Officer Gary Wagner and calling it a brutal crime. They reminded the public of the crucial roles police officers play and of the calls the police get daily: domestic disputes, assaults, thefts, robberies, neighborhood disturbance, traffic complaints... their responsibility is always to protect and serve. On the screen while these speeches were delivered, a police photo of Wagner, newly graduated from the academy, was shown. His short time as a police officer saddened even the harshest and most vocal police critics.

Although it was Saturday, Alan called a meeting of his unit. As expected, the Boston squad room was filled with emotion and adrenaline. To them, a family member had just been murdered. The loss of one officer caused everyone to step back and realize it could happen to any of them.

Alan knew it would be a difficult day... week... month... and he needed to remind them of a few things. After saying a few words about Officer Wagner, Alan continued his message, "We are in a hugely vulnerable and emotional state. This is the time to band together and remember to watch each other's back... to support each other. Don't go around blaming anyone... especially yourself... and I won't tolerate any 'what if's'... we need each other now." Alan let this sink in for a minute. "We all know that homicide is difficult to investigate especially when we have no leads. Whoever did this crime must be brought in, but we can make no mistakes, we need a solid case. I will be making assignments as more evidence is collected." Alan gave his final message. "I need all of you to be at your best so we can continue to protect and serve our city. There's always a counselor available if you need someone to talk with or for guidance. Please don't hesitate to do that. Be safe!" Alan nodded at the silent group and walked off.

Sasha hadn't been able to sleep all night. She kept remembering arriving at the crime scene, and finding Gary's body lying face down as if he were sleeping. She remembered checking for signs of life, and when she found none, she and Connie had immediately followed protocol and worked to preserve the scene and keep people back until other officers arrived with equipment. The hours had been hectic. Sasha still couldn't get the image of the blanket draped over Gary Wagner's body as he was finally carried out. Officers had lined the path from the subway entrance to the waiting ambulance, saluting the fallen officer. Sasha had stayed awake grieving for the young officer.

Detective Sharp's talk that morning was a sad reminder of the threats officers faced because of the few dangerous people they might encounter on the street. Intellectually, she knew the danger, but now her nerves were raw, and she wondered if she could continue. She'd shared this with her mother earlier because she felt an overwhelming sense of insecurity. Her mother comforted her and reminded her to focus on the higher goal, the longer view.

Being in the precinct today, Sasha tried to hide her physical and emotional exhaustion. She needed to stop the inner chatter of doubt and silence her nagging self-criticism. She had been a police officer for seven years and knew her best course was to move forward, like her mother advised.

It didn't take long for Alan to call Sasha into his office. When she arrived, he could tell she was deeply unsettled. "How are you feeling, Officer Lane?"

Attempting to hide the anxiety in her voice, Sasha answered. "I have to admit my concentration is lacking."

Alan understood. "I appreciate the work you did securing the crime scene. Your quick work established a large enough perimeter to contain the evidence and hold back the onlookers. Nice work." Alan took a moment to see Sasha's reaction. Her slight smile and nod were enough for him to continue in another direction. "Over the course of the next few days, I want you to take charge of the incoming phone calls. You know how upset the public gets until a suspect is arrested. We'll be getting a lot of calls from people trying to solve the case for us, and I believe you'll be able to create order out of the chaos." Alan noticed a look of concern on the officer's face. "I hope you understand this is not a step down and that I need your expertise to help find who did this. Any leads at all that come in, please report to me."

"Yes, sir. Do you want me to start today?"

"Only if you feel up to it. Log in for overtime and if you can come in tomorrow, too, I'd appreciate it."

"I can do that. Will someone else be assigned the phone, sir?"

"I've asked Officer Beale to be here. I believe you two will be able to handle this... just keep good records."

"Of course. Thank you." Sasha began to stand up when Alan asked her one more thing. "Do you remember anything more about your day with Officer Wagner? I know you gave a detailed account in your report, but did you notice anything that was bothering him?"

Sasha sat back down on the chair. "I've thought about that over and over. He wanted to talk about police procedure and styles of policing. To me, he seemed very conservative in his approach and attitude. I remember thinking that your new program might change his ways of looking at the challenges people face, especially on the street."

Alan nodded. "I hoped so, too. Let's keep our eyes and ears open around the station for any conversations that might involve Wagner. He might have confided in someone else about a fear or concern he felt. Can I count on you to keep this confidential?"

"Of course. If I hear anything I'll let you know."

Enrique walked into Alan's office with two large coffees. "Do you want to leave now? I think it's going to start snowing."

"Sure. Thanks for the coffee. Let me get organized, it'll be a minute." Alan wanted to check the airline schedule because the Wagner's were due to arrive in the early evening. He imagined they would be staying at their son's apartment.

Alan and Enrique had made plans to inspect Gary's apartment before their arrival. He lived in the Back Bay, in a newer building that was surrounded by older townhouses, some in good shape and others in need of repairs. When they drove up to the address, the detectives noticed a for rent sign out in front. Looking at each other, they wondered how much an apartment would cost in this area. Enrique quickly took out his phone and texted the number on the sign. "It's a two bedroom... and get this... the rent's $2200!"

Alan looked surprised. "How can people afford that? Things are so crazy right now... "

They rang for the manager and were led to an apartment on the first floor. It probably didn't have such a pricey rent since it was a one bedroom and overlooked the alley in the back. The apartment included a living room, dining area, bedroom, bathroom, and a kitchenette. It was probably around 700 square feet.

Their first impression was that Wagner was very orderly and clean, almost hygienic. His shoes were lined up at the door, and the floor was polished. When they searched the kitchen cupboards, they found several cleaning products and appliances. The sink was spotless, and all the dishes were stored according to size and color. The drawers in the bedroom dresser were equally organized and the clothes in his closet were facing the same direction and color coordinated. His queen size bed was made with crisp corners and a notepad and pen were set neatly on the nightstand.

"Well, I guess you would say he was fastidious." Enrique acknowledged.

Alan nodded slowly and looked around. "Okay... what's missing? This seems sterile and missing some common items, like books or magazines."

Enrique agreed. "He's got a TV, but no DVD's. That's interesting. Usually someone his age likes movies... or video games. Did you look in the fridge? It's all arranged by product type... fruit together... dairy together... it's kind of strange."

Alan continued to look at the empty walls. "No artwork or even photos. It feels like no one lives here."

Enrique had a thought. "I'm wondering if he's a germaphobe. Maybe that's why the shelters and encampments aroused such disgust in him."

Alan nodded. "That's the first thing that makes sense to me. If he has a fear of bacteria and germs, he would be uncomfortable meeting people who were living rough. I guess we'll find out more when his parents arrive. They should be here later today."

The men took a few photos of the rooms and then left, learning a little more about the slain officer.

Henry and Helen Wagner arrived at the precinct at 6:30. They looked and felt subdued. Clearing his throat a couple of times, Henry asked, "When can we see our son?"

Alan understood their need to confirm their son's death and had rung ahead to make certain the body was viewable. Lloyd Randell was waiting and insisted on being the one to escort the Wagner's to the autopsy room and answer any questions they might have.

Helen covered her face briefly when she saw her son lying on the table. She then bent forward and kissed his forehead while her tears flowed onto his face. Henry dug for tissues to hand his wife and then reached out to touch his son's shoulder. Any hope they had that the corpse would not be Gary, was washed away. They were there to say goodbye.

After some time, they met with Alan again in his office. He wanted to alleviate any suffering he could and offered to talk with them in the morning. "Perhaps you would feel more comfortable talking outside the precinct."

Henry looked at Helen and then agreed. "We're staying at Gary's apartment. Could we meet there?"

They decided on 10:00 the following morning.

SUNDAY, JANUARY 26TH

Connie and Sasha had worked up a template to handle the calls that were streaming into the precinct. People wanted to know where to send a card to the officer's family, where the funeral would take place, and other friendly calls. But there were also calls from people who ranted about police brutality and problems on the street. Each call had to be recorded and dealt with in a calm and reassuring manner.

Alan was surprised to see both officers on the phones when he arrived at 9:00. He walked over to talk with them between calls. "How's it going?"

Connie looked up from her writing and responded. "I had no idea that so many people wanted to get involved. Is this what usually happens?"

Alan shook his head. "Not like this. Officer Wagner was young and had recently graduated from the academy. I suppose calls are coming in from concerned citizens, either with condolences or complaints about police protection and training. Is that what you're finding?"

Both officers nodded. Sasha spoke up, "I've had a few strange calls that could be investigated. One was from a woman who said she noticed a man running by her store in the late afternoon. I asked her if it was an older guy... you know, like Vince Robarts... and she said no. It was a young guy, tall and he seemed worried."

Alan was interested. "Give me her number and I'll talk with her." He thanked the officers and then saw Enrique arrive. With a slight wave, Alan walked over to him. "Let's go meet with the Wagner's now. Hopefully, we'll beat the storm." Already, the snow that was predicted the night before had shown up with icy gusts and the streets were a mess.

Henry Wagner met them at the door of his son's apartment. Alan could smell coffee and something baking when they walked in. "Helen is hoping you would join us for coffee and scones. She always loved to make them for Gary." Both men agreed and sat at the small dinette table.

Helen looked at home serving the warm jam filled pastry and then sat down to join them. "How can we help?"

Alan took out his notebook and pen. He could tell that the older couple were exhausted and had probably not slept. He decided to ease them into the discussion. "Tell me about Gary. What was he like growing up? Who were his friends?"

Henry took a sip of coffee and then said, "Gary loved being active, especially sports. He was an accomplished basketball player and played for years. In fact, he thought he would get picked up by an NBA team one day." Henry shook his head, "I knew he wouldn't... not these days when players are close to seven feet tall. But it was a good dream."

Alan smiled. "So, he was competitive? Did you see this trait in other ways? Maybe in his schoolwork or with his friends? Did he push himself?"

Helen looked at Henry and then spoke up. "I always thought he was too hard on himself. I think it was his need to

66

control things, and he had some expectations that were far outside of his ability."

Alan was interested. "Can you give me an example?"

Helen thought for a minute. "Besides basketball, he had the tendency to fixate on small details, and needed to get things right, and sometimes he would be too rigid. We noticed how frustrated he would become and we kept telling him to enjoy everything he had achieved so far. Be patient." Helen teared up and reached for Henry's hand.

She seemed to consider something before saying, "We asked him to set realistic goals and were pleased when he decided on the police academy. We thought he would experience the discipline and order he thrived on."

Alan nodded and then shared his observations. "We noticed how tidy he kept things here. Did he have any phobias, like germs or bacteria?"

Henry smiled slightly. "We only saw that when he moved out for college. His dorm room was amazingly tidy. We teased him about it, but he insisted it was how he preferred his space."

Alan changed directions. "Did your son have a girlfriend? Someone he was close to?"

Helen spoke up quickly. "We were hoping you would tell us. Gary kept his social life private, and we thought he wasn't telling us anything until he was ready. He had a girlfriend in high school, but they went their separate ways once college started."

"Do his sisters know anything about his dating life?"

"No, they always tried to find out, but never could. Gary was just very private."

Enrique spoke up. "I noticed that he was looking

through profiles on a dating site one day. Do you know anything about that?"

Both Henry and Helen looked surprised. Henry responded, "He hated those sites. At least that's what he said when one of his sisters asked him. When was this?"

"Just last week. We're looking into it."

Alan needed more answers. "Did Gary ever have a disagreement with anyone that may have provoked them? Anyone he talked about who maybe held a grudge?"

Henry put his hand on his chin and rubbed it. "There were always spats on the basketball court, of course. But that was years ago. How about the police academy? Do they know if he had trouble with someone?"

Alan shook his head. "Not that we heard. We have his computer and phone, so we're looking into any suspicious sites or numbers."

"Will you let us know what you find?" Henry asked.

"As much as I can, but this is an ongoing investigation." Alan reminded them.

When they left the couple, Enrique asked Alan what he thought. Alan shook his head. "There's so much we don't know yet about Officer Wagner. Hopefully, his computer will fill in some of the answers. I just wonder why a close friend hasn't come forward."

The small woman walked into the precinct unnoticed. Being a short person, barely five feet tall, she was constantly aware of the conflicting issues of height since adult life was not arranged to accommodate short people. So, once more, there she was, trying to get someone's attention in a loud room filled with police officers.

Walking a few steps forward, she spotted a door that looked hopeful. Maybe that was the captain's office. Weaving her way around desks, she approached the door and gently knocked. Alan looked up from his computer and saw her standing there. His first thought was that it was a child. He stood up quickly and on second glance realized it was a grown woman. She was dressed smartly in a camel hair jacket, a navy-blue skirt and lavender blouse. Her hair was light brown, but streaks of gray were beginning to show through. Alan put out his hand and introduced himself.

"May I help you?" he questioned. "Please come in and have a seat." The woman sat on the chair next to Alan's desk and placed her designer bag on the floor. As expected, the chair did not allow her feet to touch the floor. One more annoying thing about being short.

"Thank you, Detective. My name is Marilyn Dobbs. I believe I may have some information for you about the police officer who was killed Friday."

Alan sat down behind his desk and nodded. "I would be very interested."

"I called in earlier and spoke with a very lovely officer who asked for my phone number. But since I was at the market and passing by the precinct, I thought someone might be here to take my report."

At this point Marilyn stopped. If not for effect, just to see if Alan was really interested. She was a very patient person.

"Go on, please." Alan coaxed.

"I saw the slain officer's face on the internet, and I remembered someone who looked like him in front of my store late Friday afternoon. I went through my store's CCTV tapes and my photos show two people talking with each other. In fact, it seems they were arguing."

"Did you bring the tapes with you today?"

"Yes, of course. And I printed some photos out." Marilyn reached into her bag and pulled out a folder. Alan scanned the images and realized he would have to take them to his experts to get clearer pictures.

"I appreciate this, Ms. Dobbs. Can I get the name of your store and the address so we can follow up with this location?"

"Yes, of course. I own a bookstore on State Street. It's called "The Constant Reader." Marilyn scooted forward in the chair and reached for a pen on Alan's desk. Alan quickly moved his files to the side and pulled out a post-it stack of bright yellow paper. As Marilyn wrote her number and name on the paper, Alan noticed how small and lovely her hands were. Like a child's, but graceful. She handed him the note and then stood up to leave.

Alan walked her through the squad room and wondered more about her. "Are you from Boston, Ms. Dobbs?"

"Yes," Marilyn answered. "My parents owned the bookstore for years and then gave it to me when they retired. Are you a reader Detective?"

Alan smiled. "I wish I had time to read. Maybe when I finally retire."

Marilyn nodded. "Well, when you want to find a good book, please come by the store and I'll be happy to help you find a good one."

Alan watched her walk out the door and marveled at her fast pace. She probably always had to walk quickly to keep up with taller friends and acquaintances. He'd never thought of that before.

DIANE M. McPHEE

When Alan returned to his office, Enrique was there holding a report. "I've got Wagner's phone records here. Do you want to go over them?"

"Leave it with me. Right now, I want you to go home and be with your family. And tell Officers Lane and Beale to also go home. We can pick all of this up in the morning."

As Alan watched the officers leave, he decided to make a phone call. He hadn't spoken to Maggie in over a week. She had visited him for the holidays, and he already missed her and wished they lived closer. Maggie lived on an Island in the Pacific Northwest and ran a Bed and Breakfast Inn. Looking at his watch and noting the time difference, he made the call.

"Alan! Perfect timing! I'm just enjoying a cup of tea and reading my book."

He loved this about her. She always seemed so happy to hear from him. "I wish I were there... or you here... " Alan said shyly. He always felt uncomfortable letting his feelings for anyone be apparent. "What book are you reading?"

"It's a book about an older lady and an octopus, and it takes place around here. Do you know how smart these animals are?"

"I saw a documentary on octopi a few months ago. The guy who was filming kept saying that very thing. Maybe I should read the book, too. Remind me, will you? What's new with you, and the Island?"

They spoke at length about the people he had met when he took a three month leave from the force and rented a house near her. He had met some wonderful people and unexpectedly became involved with an investigation of the murder of two teens. Drugs were involved and Maggie told him that people still talked about his speech at the town hall meeting when he spoke about drug problems. He had hoped to make them aware that drugs were everywhere you go, not just in the big cities.

Maggie continued to ask questions. "How are things in Boston? I heard the weather is freezing."

Alan told her about the icy streets and his concerns for the rough sleepers. "Maybe you heard, but one of our young officers was killed two nights ago."

"No, I hadn't heard! I was so busy over the weekend that I never got around to watching the news. What happened?"

"We're investigating. He had recently graduated from the academy, so I can't say that I knew him well. But, as you can imagine, every officer is now on alert."

"Do you have any leads?"

"No, but it's early. We're just piecing together his movements and background. I met with his parents today... you can imagine how sad that was."

"I can't imagine. Those poor people. You have such responsibility, Alan. This must get to you... when someone you supervise and care about is killed. Is there anything I can do?"

"Just be you." Alan smiled into the phone. Maggie always wanted to comfort everyone. When she visited him, they spent some time with Enrique and Marie, and both women immediately meshed. They recognized their similar natures as caregivers, and shared wonderful stories.

When Alan hung up, he realized he hadn't eaten all day. He decided to grab a salad from Whole Foods and make it an early night. He was tired, and appreciated that he had a warm home to go to... how do people survive on the street?

Raymond warmed himself by the smoldering campfire near the path of tents, bags of clothes and pots and pans... everything someone needed when they had no place else to go. Today, the rats didn't seem interested in the piles of garbage and heaps of personal possessions.

Ray, a transplant from Detroit, had been laid off from his job as a welder last year. He moved to Boston and lived in a motel for a month before deciding to buy a tent and take refuge on the street. He hoped in time to save enough money and move into more stable accommodations. He got a job with a construction company but didn't let them know he lived in the encampment. It was a good decision because Ray just found out he'll have to find another location because in a matter of weeks, everyone who camped here and everything they owned would be swept away due to safety concerns. What safety concerns? Try living in a tent!

Ray reached for the cheap bottle of vodka that always helped soothe the anger that boiled up inside him. The volunteer was around today and left it for him. He was a good guy.

MONDAY, JANUARY 27TH

I'll bet you fifty bucks it's not true!" Alan heard the two officers yelling as he walked into the squad room. Stopping at the door, and out of sight from the arguing, Alan tried to make out what the commotion was about.

"It *is* true! You can ask any medical pro about it! Arsenic poisoning can be mistaken for simple influenza." The officer's voices were loud, and Alan recognized it to be an experienced officer and a young recruit. He would have to be careful not to make judgements, but he needed to interfere and calm everyone down.

Just as he was about to step into the room, Alan heard a familiar voice. "Either way, poisoners are hard to catch and even harder to convict." Enrique continued, "And, in the long run, any homicidal poisoning requires calculating intelligence."

Alan entered the room. "Speaking of poisoning, I remember reading about an interesting case when a man almost got away with poisoning his wife of twenty years. He kept adding poison to her nightly cocktail and over the course of a few months, she died of what looked like a heart attack. No one thought anything of it until the husband demanded that a required autopsy *not* be performed. That made the police suspicious, so they got a court order to allow the

75

autopsy and they found arsenic swirling through the woman's every organ."

He let that sink in and then said, "The primary reason for arsenic's popularity is that when it's mixed with food or drink, it's difficult to taste. It could be added to soup, liquor or even a hot cup of coffee."

Alan looked at the officers who had been arguing. "Why is this even coming up? Is there a suspicious poisoning?"

The older officer was quick to reply. "Detective, we've been hearing about several homeless people getting sick and some even dying from some kind of unexplained illness. They complain about cramps in their legs and getting fidgets in their hands and feet, like pins and needles. It just seems suspicious to me and I'm wondering if someone is trying to poison people."

Alan looked surprised. This was the first he'd heard of an illness spreading through the camps. "I'll have someone follow up on this. Thanks for letting me know."

Enrique followed Alan into his office. "Do you want me to follow up on this? I guess there's always new opportunities for clever poisoners."

Alan gathered his thoughts for a minute. "From what I know, poisoners are cold, calculating and slightly inhuman perpetrators. Most of these criminals get away with murder because few witnesses come forward with information, usually out of fear of being poisoned themselves."

Enrique agreed. "Unfortunately, if someone is targeting the homeless population, what we might consider natural causes from the elements could be a cold-blooded murder."

Alan felt more agitation than usual because he now had another line of inquiry to investigate. "Let me think about it. If something suspicious is going on in the camps, it might escalate if we don't investigate, but right now, our priority is to find out who killed Officer Wagner."

Alan called down to the pathology lab to talk with Lloyd Randell. "Lloyd... any news on our officer?"

Lloyd let out a long sigh. "It was definitely a homicide. It looks like he put up a fight... bruises on his hands and legs. He was beaten up, but it was the strangulation that killed him. From what I can tell, it was some kind of a cord, leaving marks like an extension cord. Anyone could have one and to my knowledge, nothing like that was found in the area. The perp was probably tall, but I can't have any sort of measurements for a day or two. I've taken some skin from under Gary's fingernails that I've sent to the lab. That's about it. Any news your way?"

"No, not yet. But let me ask you something, have you heard anything about poisonings going on in the encampments? Or illnesses that people are worried about?"

"Not that I know of. I'll ask around."

The men rang off and Alan looked at Enrique. "Close the door, please."

Enrique turned to the door and then sat next to Alan's desk. He took out his notebook. "Ready."

"Like I said, our number one priority is to find Officer Wagner's killer. I have IT going through some CCTV on the streets by the tunnel, and a woman came in yesterday with tapes from her shop that look like Wagner was arguing with someone. We'll know more today when the photos are uploaded and processed. I want you to go through his phone records and computer history to see what you can find. Officer Wagner had to have some friends he hung out with.

Has anyone here said anything about this?"

Enrique shook his head. "Nobody. I hate to say it, but he could be annoying. Officers who rode with him said he liked to talk smack... you know... make critical and insulting comments about people. He liked the reaction he got."

"That sounds immature and inappropriate, especially for an officer. Maybe he thought he was witty."

"I suppose. But it could get under someone's skin enough to maybe want to rough him up."

"We need to know his daily movements. When he wasn't at work, what did he do? Who did he meet? Let me know what you find out from his cell and computer."

"What about this poison thing? Do you want me to investigate it?"

"No. I'm going to have Officer Beale and Officer Lane take that on. I'll be putting two other officers on phone duty."

Sasha was surprised to be put on another assignment, but it was a bonus to be partnered with Connie again. They had both overheard the argument about possible arsenic poisoning and admitted they knew very little on the subject. They would need some time to work out a plan of action and educate themselves on poisons. But first, they decided to visit the downtown shelter and confirm that an illness might have spread throughout some of the camps.

Deacon Levi Martin was surprised to see the officers enter the shelter. He had read about the Officer being killed, but it didn't have anything to do with anyone he knew. "I'm sorry for your loss... the police officer who was killed." He looked at the women with anticipation, hoping they had found the killer.

Sasha replied, "We're all on alert. But we're here for another reason. It's come to our attention that there's an illness that's quite serious invading the homeless population. Do you know anything about this?"

Levi looked concerned and nodded. "We've had some people overcome by something that's maybe even caused some deaths. Of course, we consider every possibility, because folks here are often suffering with chronic conditions that are life-threatening. Should we be worried?"

Connie and Sasha shook their heads. Sasha spoke up, "Not yet. We're going to investigate the camps and other shelters to learn more. We just don't want a deadly virus circulating, especially if we can get on top of it. In the meantime, call the station if you hear anything."

Levi still looked worried. "Are you thinking it could be poison?"

The officers looked at each other. They didn't want a rumor to be running through the communities. "We're currently just curious, and we don't want to worry people. Please keep this to yourself." Sasha handed Levi her card and wanted to look around the building while Connie asked to see the names of those who were regulars at the shelter.

While Enrique waited for the tech department to give him the CCTV photos, he thought some more about the crime scene. Vince Robarts had been riding the subway because of the harsh weather report, and he admitted to hiding in storage spaces on days when the weather was cold. Most street people knew that subway hiding places were reachable by walking along the tracks to find empty storage rooms suitable for sleeping or even partying, and they could steer clear of

Transit cops after the subway closed at 1:00am.

At the time of the murder, officers had searched all the storage units along the track, hoping that something would lead them to the killer. But so far, they had learned nothing.

Enrique shook his head in frustration. What was Officer Wagner doing there? This wasn't his train home, so he must have been following up on something or going to meet with someone.

In the back of his mind, Alan still needed to figure out why he had a 3:00 reminder on the receipt he found in his pocket. Looking at his watch, he realized he had two hours to remember some appointment or meeting. Just to be certain it didn't involve his son, he decided to give Sam a quick call.

"Hey, Dad... what's up?" Sam always asked the same question whenever Alan called.

"I suppose you heard about an officer being killed last week... I'm working on that. What are you up to?"

"Yeah... I'm sorry to hear about the officer. He was one of yours, right?"

"Yes. And he was young. Hopefully we'll find the killer soon."

"Are you coming to the game today?"

That was it! The basketball tournament! Sam had wanted him to come watch a game he coached because his team had the opportunity to move on to the playoffs. "Yes... three, right?"

"Yeah. It's at the gym by my office. Even if you make it for the last half, it should be a good match."

"Okay. I'll see you there." Alan rang off and let out a sigh of relief. Now he remembered when Sam had taken out a receipt and wrote down the time for him. It all made sense because Sam was painting his apartment and that's why the message was on the hardware store receipt. He looked at his phone and told himself he needed to figure out how to use the calendar to set alarms as reminders. Hopefully, it wouldn't be that hard.

Alan remembered his promise to keep in touch with the Wagners. Maybe this would be a good opportunity to meet with them, especially since their apartment and the location of the gym were both in the Back Bay. He called and found out they were available.

When Alan arrived at 2:30, Henry Wagner opened the door and immediately asked, "Any news?"

Alan shook his head. "I'm afraid not. We're going through your son's phone and computer, hoping to find something to connect him to a person or persons. I just have a few more questions for you."

Henry led Alan into the living room where Helen was sitting. She nodded but did not offer a smile. Alan couldn't blame her; grief is a terrible companion. Alan began his questions. "Are your daughters by any chance coming to meet you here?"

"No, they're waiting for us to bring their brother home for a funeral. Why?" Henry was concerned.

"I thought I might be able to talk with them and see if they knew more about Gary. Sometimes siblings are more aware of each other's personal lives. For instance, we haven't heard from anyone who knew Gary outside of the precinct. It seems odd that someone hasn't come forward yet."

Helen looked at Henry. "We agree. When your child moves away from home you just imagine he has all the friends and contacts he needs. We only saw him twice or three times a year, and he always seemed happy. He talked about the academy and then the police station. What do you think this means?"

"Well, one consideration is that he was a loner. He didn't seem to hang out with other officers at the station, but we could be wrong. The other is that he wanted his life to stay private. Maybe he felt he would be judged or restricted in some ways. Even now, with everyone trying to accept beliefs and personal space, some people still can't share a different lifestyle."

Henry shook his head in disagreement. "Gary was the straightest guy around. He wasn't gay if that's what you mean. He always had friends. This is all a mystery to us... especially that he didn't have a lot of friends around here."

"So, no one has come around and no cards or letters have arrived?" Alan gently asked.

"No. Nothing. Not even anyone in this complex." Henry looked to Helen to confirm this.

"My officers will be knocking on some doors this week to talk to people in the area. Don't worry if you see them." Alan thought for a minute. "Which one of Gary's sisters was he closest to?"

Helen thought for a minute. "Wendy is... was... his favorite. She's a couple years older and they always did things together. Do you want to talk with her?"

"Yes. Please give me her number." It was agreed that they would have Wendy call Alan. She was terribly upset about losing her brother and might need some time before she made the call.

Alan stood to leave. Once again, he looked at the

spotless apartment and wondered how someone kept a space so neat.

By the time Alan got home after the basketball game, he poured himself a glass of red wine and sat in his old recliner. Sam's team had won, and he was delighted to see how much the players loved Sam. Alan even got to talk with Abby, Sam's girlfriend, during the game. She also seemed to love Sam. Alan smiled just thinking about it.

The snow was piling up.

An older lady stirred the worn fry pan over the makeshift burner and shook her head. "I guess that illness I had affected my taste too because I can only taste lemons and sometimes... if I'm lucky... sweets."

The man, who claimed to be a volunteer, looked at the size of the woman who must weigh close to three hundred pounds. He thought to himself that if you can't taste food, what would be the point of eating so much. But where does this woman get all the food to maintain her large weight? Drinking is a weight gainer, maybe she drinks cheap beer all day. She probably just sits on her fat rear, too.

"I know what you're thinking... that I'm fat... " The woman bent over the pan full of some sort of stew and tried to smell the contents. "I still do this... try to smell it... it's a habit, I guess. But sometimes I get just a whiff and I'm so happy." She smiled and the man could see that her front two teeth were missing.

"So, you're able to enjoy food you cannot taste." He was attempting to make polite conversation, but his mind was calculating how much he needed to apply for such a large woman.

"Oh, I can't say I'm thrilled about it. I just try and remember what it tastes like, especially my favorites like burgers and fried chicken."

The man walked away disgusted by this woman and all the people he saw crouching near shops. There was only one way to eliminate the homeless. It was up to him.

TUESDAY, JANUARY 28TH

Alan sent two officers to Gary's apartment complex early in the day to interview surrounding neighbors and attempt to learn more about Wagner. He then called Connie and Sasha into his office to see how the investigation on the homeless was playing out.

Sasha took out her notes. "We interviewed Levi Martin at the shelter and asked about any illness he might know that could be running through the camps. He said there might be some suspicious deaths, but it was hard to determine because of the chronic illnesses people suffered with." She looked to Connie for agreement.

Connie shook her head slightly. "There seems to be a secret pact among the people who volunteer... you know... maybe because they're aware of all the drugs and alcohol people need to survive on the street. They don't want to say anything. I think we need to interview people who are themselves homeless, but who act as confidants or partners to others. Maybe they'll give us an idea of what's going on."

Alan nodded. "Good plan. If you can find one or a couple of concerned people, they may be worried enough to talk. Continue this line of thinking and get back with me."

Enrique walked into the office as the women were leaving. "I've got the phone records from Wagner's cell. It looks like he made very few calls. This makes me think he had another phone… especially if he had some sort of secret life going."

Alan related the conversation he had with the Wagners. Just then his phone rang. "Detective Sharp."

It was Wendy Wagner, Gary's sister. Alan held up his hand to Enrique indicating he would get back with him and to close the door.

"Detective, you wanted to speak with me about my brother?" Wendy's voice sounded quiet and restrained.

"Thank you for calling. I'm very sorry about what happened to Gary. We're working to find the culprit and make an arrest. I was wondering, Wendy, if you knew of any friends or relationships that Gary had. We can't seem to locate a number for anyone."

Wendy hesitated. "Gary was very private about relationships. Even though he seemed to have an outgoing side, he had difficulty connecting with people on a personal level. You probably already know he developed almost a compulsive need for structure and order, and that didn't help him meet someone. Did you know he was seeing a therapist?"

Alan was surprised. Police usually have an aversion to seeking help. This was a good lead. "Did he tell you who he was seeing?"

"Not their name. It was someone in your area because he mentioned it was close to the precinct. The last time I spoke with him, he said the therapist was helping."

"I'm wondering, did he have another phone besides the one we found?"

"I'm not sure. When he called me on another line, I thought it was from the station."

Now Alan had more to go on. "Wendy, we have an idea that he was searching online dating sites. Did you know this?"

Wendy let out a long sigh. "No. I wish he would have confided in me more. When he was home for Christmas, I caught him calling someone and my intuition told me it was for a date. I know he seemed happier while he was here, and I wish I would have asked him if he was seeing someone."

"This has been a big help, Wendy. Can I call you again if I have more questions? And will you call me if you think of anything important?"

"Yes, Detective, I promise I will."

When they hung up, Alan sat for a moment with the new information. If Gary was seeing a therapist, he would have to find out who it was. There might be another phone to locate, too. He called Enrique back into his office.

Doctor Erik Stanton was saddened when he heard that his patient, Gary Wagner, had been killed. He had expected the police to find his number on Gary's contact list, but so far, he hadn't been contacted. As a counselor, he was bound by secrecy and wouldn't be able to give them too much information on his client, but he had been seeing Gary for over six months and probably knew more than anyone.

Gary's case was complicated. He had acute anxiety that could be diagnosed as borderline personality disorder. He appeared to others as capable and outgoing, but he was plagued with severe anxiety about conflicts. To hide this, he maintained a façade of hyper-competence and independence.

Dr. Stanton knew Gary felt instability in relationships because he viewed things in extremes, such as only good or bad. For example, Gary saw his parents as nurturing, but then spoke about how cruelly punitive they were when it came to giving him any freedom. These shifts reflected a disillusionment and fear of rejection. Dr. Stanton believed that psychodynamic therapy might help Gary understand certain patterns in his life, especially involving relationships, emotions, and behaviors.

He felt they had been making progress and exploring avenues to healthy emotional outlets. They had discussed music, breathing exercises, and even taking long showers as strategies to deal with negative situations and emotions that come up. Those situations usually involved the people he worked with. Gary had the opinion that by being clever and joking around, he would win over his team. But sometimes this kind of behavior at work goes too far. Dr. Stanton wondered if maybe Gary offended the wrong person.

By noon, the officers who interviewed people in Gary's apartment complex returned to the precinct and met with Alan.

"We talked with the neighbors who lived on the same floor. One older lady was upset to learn that Officer Wagner had been killed. She said he was a good neighbor and often offered to carry her groceries for her. Another man two doors down said the officer was never home. He seldom heard or saw him. We knocked on several doors and got no response. I think people were already gone or saw our car and just didn't answer. Then we went to the convenience store that was nearby. The owner said that Officer Wagner came in a couple times a week. When we asked what he bought, he said usually snack food and sometimes beer. We asked if he was ever with anyone, and the guy said no. Never."

Alan shook his head. "There must be more. How could someone be so off the radar from people he lived next door to? Okay, I want you to go back and talk with people who are available once they get home from work. And try to get more information from the manager. When we spoke with him on Saturday, he didn't say much."

Alan's phone rang, and when he looked at the caller ID he smiled. "Sidney! How are you doing?"

"Alan, I just got back from a conference and saw that one of your officers had been killed. What do you know so far?" Sidney only asked as a friend, not as legal help. If Alan needed him to look into something, he would find a way without getting his law firm involved.

"I wish I knew more. Officer Wagner's life seems to be elusive in many ways. We're in the early stages... trying to run down leads. I guess he had a second phone to make personal calls, and we're trying to locate that now. His sister told me he was seeing a counselor in the area, so I need to find out who that was, too. You know how this goes... two steps forward... and then back a couple."

The men spoke some more and then made plans to meet later in the week for a meal. Alan knew how lucky he was to have such a good friend. Especially at this age when everyone seemed to be more isolated. This made him wonder again why no one had claimed to be a friend of Officer Wagner's.

Sasha sat in the car with Connie and scanned the encampment by the bridge. They had been to three other camps, but nobody wanted to talk with them about an illness or being sick. Now they were waiting to find someone named

Trevor who was supposed to be a mentor for several rough sleepers. The officers were told he made daily rounds through the camps to check on people and bring supplies from the clinic. Not meds, but bandages, cleaning astringents, and other first aid needs. He was trusted by everyone and always called people by their first names as he listened carefully when they unloaded their stories.

All they knew was that he was a big guy, wearing a red knit hat and carrying a green backpack. "Over there… " Sasha said. She and Connie got out of the car and slowly walked towards the man who had just entered the camp.

"Mr. Trevor… can we have a minute?" Connie called out.

Trevor turned when he heard his name being called. When he saw who it was, he held his breath for a minute. Why were the police here? Eyeing them carefully, he asked, "What do you want? I'm busy right now."

The officers understood his guardedness and knew he was at the camp to help, and that he took his work seriously. Connie nodded respectfully and said, "We know you're busy. We just need a few minutes. It's about a medical situation in the camps we're following up on."

That got Trevor's attention. He walked over to the officers and offered his hand. When both women shook it, he motioned to a bench across the street. "Let's go there and talk. We'll have more privacy."

Sasha began the questioning. "Have you heard about an illness that's running through the camp? Like an influenza that's making people very sick."

Trevor nodded and pulled the hat off his head. He had long curly auburn hair that stuck close to his head and face. In a way, he was attractive, but maybe that was because of his dark hazel eyes that seemed warm and intelligent. "I've been concerned. There've been instances where people are gasping for air and vomiting over and over. It seems more like food poisoning than a sickness like the flu. Sometimes it lasts for hours and a few of my mates have passed out. Do you know what's going on?"

The women shook their heads. Connie spoke up, "Is there someone you know who's sick right now? We could take them to the ER and get them tested."

Trevor nodded. "Over in the third tent," he pointed across the street. "A woman's been sick since yesterday. She might decide to go with you and get treated. Her name's Ruth."

The officers thanked Trevor and asked him to introduce them to Ruth. When they approached the tent, they could already smell a rotting odor and human waste. Trevor shook his head and opened the tent flap. "Ruth? How are you feeling?"

A moan came from the interior. When the officers peered into the tent, they saw a large woman who was lying on her side, unable to sit up or even to move. They called for an ambulance and waited.

The volunteer heard the ambulance and watched as it approached the camp. He thought he had given enough of the stuff to the fat female to kill her. It could have killed a horse! He didn't plan on an ambulance and cops. He would have to be more careful.

At 5:15, officers were back at the apartment units, trying to find someone who knew Officer Wagner. After several tries, a young teenage girl answered a door on the lower floors. When she saw the officers, she took a step back. "Mom... you better come to the door."

Cheryl Nelson had just returned home from work after picking up her daughter and son from their school activities. "Can I help you?" she asked cautiously.

"Madam, we're investigating the death of a tenant in the building. Did you know Gary Wagner?"

"The officer, right?" Cheryl looked at each of them, her eyes darting back and forth.

"That's right. He lived a few doors down from you and we're wondering how well you might have known him."

Cheryl put a hand to her mouth and shook her head. "I really didn't know him. I just knew he was a policeman and felt safer because he lived here. I talked with him a few times in passing and told him just that. When you have young kids, you need all the protection you can get."

"Did you notice if he ever had company visiting him? Did you see him with anyone?"

The young girl was listening and spoke up, "I did. I saw him with a lady a couple of times."

"What did she look like?"

"She was pretty. She was... um... not black... but brown skin and curly black hair. And she was short... because he was so tall."

The officers were writing this new information down. "When did you see them together?"

"Last week. I don't remember what day. But it was after I got home from school. I had to go to the store, and I saw them."

The officers glanced around the building for any cameras. They thanked the teen and her mother, and decided it was time to talk with the manager.

Ralph Macdonald was sweeping the apartment steps when the officers appeared. He had noticed them earlier and hoped they would leave the premises before people started to get worried and call him. "What do you need? Is this about Wagner?"

"Yes. Do you have CCTV cameras around the building? Maybe ones that oversee the parking lot?"

"Yeah… sure. I guess it's okay. What day do you need? I usually erase everything after a week or two."

"Let's have everything you've saved."

Macdonald walked quickly into his office and got to work on the cameras. Ten minutes later he returned with copies and handed them over to the officers. He didn't want to ask too many questions but wanted to help. "Anything else?"

"Not so far. But thanks." The officers left and drove immediately to the precinct.

WEDNESDAY, JANUARY 29TH

Connie and Sasha met Alan at the office early to report on the suspected poisoning at the homeless camp. They had followed the ambulance to Mass General and when they finally left, the woman was still in the ICU with a 50-50 chance of recovery.

Sasha consulted her notes. "Dr. Leisha Meyers said it was likely arsenic poisoning. The victim, her name is Ruth, was almost unconscious when we found her. Food and drink from her tent were sent to the lab and we're waiting to hear the results. But the signs seem clear to the doctor. Which means the rumors might be true and there could be a crazed arsenic killer roaming the homeless camps."

Alan nodded. "Give me the number for the doctor. I want to see if there's a comparison between the symptoms she found, and some other stories from the camps. Things aren't always obvious with poisoning. One thing I know about arsenic is there needs to be a high enough dose to kill someone but low enough to fool the victims." Alan dialed the doctor.

Dr. Leisha Meyers called Alan back an hour later. She got right to the point. "Detective, I understand you want to investigate the cause of my patient's alleged poisoning."

"Yes, Doctor. We need to know the specifics of this kind

of poison. Are you certain she was poisoned?"

"Her symptoms seem clear: nausea and vomiting, an abnormal heart rhythm, and complaints of muscle cramps. We quickly obtained blood samples, but it was her urine sample that helped us with the diagnosis. It was white arsenic, probably ground fine so it was undetectable in her food. We have our lab testing what we found at her place to be certain."

"Tell me Doctor, how would someone know if they were exposed to arsenic poison?"

"Specifically, because white arsenic mixes beautifully with foods it will hide the faint metallic taste. Ground extra fine into baked goods, though, it's almost undetectable. The one thing people do complain about is a sandy feel in their mouth... gritty... a rough texture. And given in high enough doses, the obvious symptoms occur in about twenty minutes."

Alan thanked the doctor and sat thinking about his next move. If it's true that someone was secretly poisoning a specific population, it was an amoral act, malicious and intentional. They could easily disappear but might develop a lust for murder because they got away with it. Unfortunately, knowing the poison was helpful, but now he had to find the poisoner. That was going to be harder.

Alan called Sasha and Connie into his office once again. "I just spoke with Doctor Meyers, and she confirmed that the people suffering from these symptoms were likely given arsenic poison. I want you to continue this investigation. Poisoners usually remain hidden and thoughtfully plan their murders. They trick people into swallowing the poison, knowing what it will do... and doing it anyway. Begin at the camps and keep your ears open to everything. We need to look for someone with motive to kill. Needless to say, it means following every clue you hear or find."

When the officers left his office, Alan called HR to find the names of local therapists. If Gary Wagner was seeing someone, he may have learned of a near-by person from the police health providers. While waiting on hold to be connected, Alan wrote a list of questions that needed to be answered. Why was Wagner talking to a counselor? Who was the woman seen with Gary at his apartment? How would they find her? How come they didn't know who his friends were? Were the apartment building's CCTV tapes ready to view? Who was he arguing with on the street in front of the bookstore? Alan underlined the last question because he had dropped the ball on that.

HR gave him the names and numbers of four therapists who worked nearby. One was a woman, and Alan suspected Gary would not have consulted with a female. He dialed the other three numbers and left a message. Fifteen minutes later Dr. Erik Stanton returned his call.

"Hello, Detective. Yes, I was seeing Gary Wagner. I'm terribly sorry to hear what happened to him. How can I be of assistance?"

"Thank you for calling, Doctor. If you have time today, I'd like to speak with you personally."

Alan could hear the clicking of a computer and knew the man was checking his schedule. "How about 4:00 today. I'm sure you have my address."

The men hung up and Alan wanted to consider another avenue to explore. One thing Gary had loved was basketball. He attended USC years ago, and Alan wondered if the coach was still available. The university was in Columbia, South Carolina, and the basketball team was called the Gamecocks. Named for fighting birds? Alan didn't follow college ball and had no idea how the school ranked, but if it were up to him, they might choose a different symbol. He shook his head and then found an email for the current basketball coach and sent him an inquiry on Wagner. Hopefully, someone might remember him as a player.

By the time Enrique walked into Alan's office, it was already past 1:00. Both men had skipped lunch and decided to order in while reviewing the investigations. Food delivery was fast and convenient, and they had a favorite delivery driver.

Enrique spread out the computer printouts from Gary's phone records and emails. It looked like he had been communicating with someone whose address was zoems9@gmail.com. "From the messages sent back and forth it appears they only recently started emailing. The messages go back a couple weeks."

"Are there any photos? Text messages?"

"No. Like I said, it seems they just started communicating. We still haven't located another phone for Gary, but we should have a lead later today. I just wonder why he needed two phones."

Alan told Enrique about meeting with the therapist at 4:00. "Maybe he can shed some light on this. What about the bookstore CCTV photos? Anything?"

"I have them here. It looks like the person of interest is facing away from the camera. We have a good photo of Gary, and he seems to be having quite an argument with this guy. Then they both walk quickly away."

As they looked through the photos, a knock on the door

revealed the driver delivering their lunch. Elizabeth, always efficient, rushed in with three bags, rubbing her hands together to warm them. "Hi guys! I wish I would've worn a couple more layers today… it's so cold out there. How's your day going?"

"Busy as usual, Elizabeth. How about you?"

"You're my last order. I get to go home now and warm up."

"Lucky you!" Enrique quipped.

Alan seemed more concerned, "Drive carefully. We depend on you, even on these icy days."

Elizabeth gave a little salute and rushed out.

The men settled in to eat and continued their investigation concerns.

Alan arrived a few minutes early for his meeting with Dr. Stanton. The waiting room was attractively furnished with four easy chairs and a subdued Persian carpet. Sports and Travel magazines were neatly stacked on end tables and a colorful map of the world was displayed on the wall. Alan wondered if this print gave people a desire for future experiences or even wanderlust as they waited for their counselor. Maybe he should get a map and begin to think about travel.

Dr. Stanton entered the room and introduced himself to Alan. He was dressed impeccably in grey slacks, a navy-blue button-down shirt, and a paisley tie. His hair was trimmed neatly and was just beginning to show grey on the sides, which made it difficult to guess his age. He was Alan's height and walked with a fast pace as he led to his office.

The office matched the waiting room with a beautifully textured rug and comfortable chairs. The Doctor sat in one chair and pointed to Alan to sit across from him. "How can I help, Detective?"

"I realize you have confidential information on Gary Wagner, but I'd like to know a few things, if possible. Did you think that Gary was in any danger? Did he speak of being worried or fearful of anyone?"

The doctor took a minute to think about the answer. He was not going to break any confidence because the law protected his sessions with a client. But since there was an ongoing investigation, he wanted to help with any information he could. "My understanding was that Gary worried more about his approach to people than about someone threatening him."

"Can you give me an example?"

"You've probably come to some conclusions yourself, Detective. I'm sure you've been to his apartment and noticed how sanitized it appeared, and you might have concluded that Gary suffered from some phobia to germs. I can confirm that he felt a need to control that area of his life, and we spoke about his anxiety surrounding it."

Alan nodded. "Yes, we noticed. We also knew his aversion to being around people who were homeless. He had very conservative views and wasn't afraid to speak up about them. I sent him out to a shelter and encampments with another detective and he was noticeably uncomfortable. Did he bring this up?"

"Yes, he did. He felt he had gone too far and should have been more careful to hide his negative feelings about street people. But, Detective, I want you to know that Gary had a good heart."

Alan appreciated that the doctor cared so much about

his patient. "Speaking of that, was he seeing anyone... have a relationship with a certain woman?"

"In our last session he told me he had met someone online. I don't know her name, but they were taking things slow. I believe he might have been keeping something from me. Maybe she was younger... or of a different race... or even older."

"We have confirmation that he was seen with a woman who was believed to be of mixed race. Would he have kept that from you?"

"Perhaps. You know, he's from a small Southern town. Race could probably be an issue if he introduced someone of color to his family. I'm certain we would have discussed this in time."

Alan nodded. "Is there anything else you can tell me?"

"I've reviewed my notes, and nothing has come up. We met twice a month and only recently began to deal with personal issues. That's how it goes, Detective. Therapy is a slow journey."

Alan thanked the doctor and asked to exchange business cards. When he left the office, he didn't know much more about Officer Wagner. But if it was true that he had issues with anxiety, maybe that's the reason he came off so abrasive to people. Maybe when they find this woman, she might offer more insight.

THURSDAY, JANUARY 30TH

A lan looked at the first thing on his list that morning and made a call to the USC basketball coach. He was put on hold, listening to NPR give the latest scandal report, when someone finally came on the line. "This is Coach Newland; how can I help you?"

"I'm Detective Sharp from the Boston Police Department and one of your players from years ago has been a member of my squad. Gary Wagner... do you remember him?"

"Yes, I was his coach." Alan heard the man breathe a long sigh. "I heard he's been killed. We're all so sorry to hear that."

"I was hoping to find out a little more about Gary's friends and relationships when you coached him. Was he a popular kid? Have a lot of friends?"

"Well, now, that's an interesting question. Gary was a good player, but he never actually played a whole game. I know that disappointed him, but in those four years we had some mighty good players. He did go on to play internationally and I heard he did fine. As for his friends, there were a couple of guys he hung out with, but I wasn't privy to any girlfriend."

"Do you remember the guys he was friends with… their names?"

"No, Detective, I really can't say. I could guess, I suppose, but I'd hate to be wrong and send you to talk with someone not involved. This was like… eight to ten years ago."

"I understand. You have my number if you think of anyone who might remember Gary. Thank you."

Alan crossed the coach off his list and started thinking. After college, Wagner went to play international and then onto the police academy. If he was twenty-eight years old at the time, maybe he was searching for a more stable lifestyle and planned to settle down. Alan's thoughts were interrupted by a knock on his office door.

"There's a woman here to see you, Detective," an officer said.

"Who?" Alan hoped to at least have a name before he met her.

"She wouldn't give me a name, just that it was about Officer Wagner."

Alan stood and followed the other officer into the squad room to meet the person. He was taken by surprise when a lovely East Asian woman, dressed in a tangerine tunic and white bloused pants, nodded his way. Her dark hair was wrapped in a bright turquoise silk scarf and as he approached, her huge golden eyes peered up at him. He introduced himself and invited her into his office. Alan pointed to the chair beside his desk and then retreated to his old swivel chair.

"My name is Zoe Singh," she began, "and Gary was my friend." Tears began to roll down her face as she reached for the Kleenex on Alan's desk. "I would like to help you, if I can."

Stunned with this information, Alan began to question

her. "Can you tell me how you knew him?"

Zoe struggled with her tears and began her story.

"Gary was a customer at the restaurant my parents own. I waitress there in between classes, and one day we started to talk. He liked Indian food and wanted to learn more about the spices and our country. Soon he was showing up a couple times a week, and we became friends."

"Where is your restaurant located, Ms. Singh?"

"Please call me Zoe, Detective. We have a small place near Cambridge. It's a very good location because of the college and tourists."

"When was the last time you saw Officer Wagner?"

Zoe glanced at Alan sadly. "He came into the restaurant last week, on Wednesday. I always enjoyed his visits, but my parents did not want me to be friends with him."

Alan thought for a moment. "Why do you say this?"

"They are very traditional people. One day my mother looked on my phone and saw the text messages Gary and I sent to each other. She became very upset and restricted our communication. But we kept in touch and would occasionally meet for coffee or lunch." Zoe looked down at her hands and quietly said, "I didn't know what happened until my father showed me the internet article that Gary had been killed. And then he gave me the strangest look... " At this point Zoe let her tears flow.

Alan walked to the water cooler and brought back a small cup of water for Zoe. This lovely gentle woman probably knew more about Gary than maybe anyone.

"Are you worried that your father might have done some harm to Gary?"

"That's the thing, when I saw the article, I remembered

that my father had been gone that Friday. It was strange because it's always a busy day, and we needed his help. We had argued lately about many things, so I assumed I had made him unhappy about something and he needed a break." Zoe hung her head and stared at the floor.

"I see... " Alan had to decide how to handle this information. He would like to question Zoe's father but didn't want to give away the confidence of what he just heard. "I think what I'll do, Miss Singh... Zoe... is visit your restaurant and ask your father some questions. I'll tell him that I knew Officer Wagner ate meals there and wondered if he noticed anyone following him or arguing with him. You don't need to be there, in fact, it would be better if you were away. What day do you have off?"

"I only work half of the day, usually from three to seven. Those are our busiest hours."

"Good. I'll come in for lunch tomorrow. Can I ask you a few questions about Gary?"

"Yes, of course."

"Was Gary worried about anything or anyone? Did he think he was in some sort of trouble?"

With a downcast expression, Zoe seemed to weigh her response. "Gary seemed anxious at times, and I thought it had to do with his job. I know he was frustrated when there was a reaction from the public that was confrontational or abusive... he said he felt hostility almost every day. He worried about his safety and complained that most people don't understand the risks and challenges police face." Zoe hesitated for a moment, maybe trying to decide if she should continue.

Alan wanted to coax her along. "Can you tell me more?"

Zoe raised her eyes, trying to think how to say this. "I think he felt a lot of confusion. Like for instance, if he faced a situation where doing the morally right thing would require breaking a department rule, he wasn't sure what he would do."

"Did he give you an example?"

Zoe looked down at her hands and spoke quietly. "One time he was on duty with another officer who had been drinking. Instead of reporting him, he kept quiet and only insisted on driving that day. He worried about it being found out and that he'd be disciplined."

"I see. Did he give you any other scenarios?"

"Well, he worried he might be called out due to an excessive force complaint. He believed that when citizens were behaving badly, or verbally abusive, and even sometimes physically combative, a more aggressive tactic was necessary."

This was all good information for Alan to be aware of. If Wagner was feeling frustrated and, perhaps, anxious, about his job, he might have put himself in a dangerous position.

Alan looked at Zoe and nodded. "I appreciate what you've just told me. This gives me more to consider. One more question, did Gary have some friends who he hung out with? Did he go to a gym or belong to a group of any sort?"

"I don't know the names of any friends. We'd been seeing each other for only three months. Sorry."

Alan thanked Zoe and asked to have her phone number. He stood to indicate the interview had ended, and as he watched her leave, he felt troubled with this new information.

Alan sat back down at his desk and gave this some thought. Being a policeman was hard work and it changes you. You need to be a problem solver and yet self-reliant. A team player and yet ready to make your own decisions. It was a complex job. Officers had to chase criminals and put themselves in dangerous situations, but also show respect and kindness to citizens. They were expected to act as though they could handle anything they encountered but they witnessed more sorrow, death, and turmoil than ordinary citizens ever see. Alan knew there were officers who needed more coaching on how to handle public confrontation with a lot more show of empathy. But he believed they all needed to be reminded to de-personalize the situations they came across and be more proactive... try harder to understand the lives and struggles of others. Alan also thought this was the right approach when dealing with the homeless population.

Connie and Sasha were at the hospital talking with Ruth about the days leading up to her serious illness. She was out of ICU and had been given a blood transfusion which made her more alert. "When can I have some food?" she grumbled. Since she was at the hospital, she expected the food to be better than anything she experienced on the street.

Sasha looked at her chart and said, "Lunch will be at 12:00. Ruth, did you realize you were poisoned?"

Ruth nodded and tried to lift her large body up without success. "It's hard to talk to you lying down like this. Can you scoot the bed up?"

Sasha raised the bed. "Ruth, let's talk about what you ate on Friday. Is that when you got so sick?"

"I been sick for days! I thought it was the croup or something... couldn't keep anything down."

"Did someone give you food that tasted odd?

Smelled bad?"

"Well... see... that's the thing. I can't smell! And I can't taste! So how would I know if it tasted or smelt bad?"

Connie intervened. "Can you remember if anyone dropped off food at your tent last week? Is that how you get your food sometimes? Someone brings it to you?"

Ruth let out a muffled laugh. "I get it anyway I can. Volunteers bring bags of food sometimes. I can't remember what day they show up."

Connie looked at Sasha and then asked, "Is it the same volunteer every time?"

"Heck no! Those do-gooders don't stick around long... volunteers see how we live and then take off!" Ruth pushed the call button for a nurse. "I'm darn hungry!"

The officers decided to leave her and not deal with explanations about diets and food selection. They knew Ruth would be upset when she heard the restrictions placed on her. Their next meeting was with Dr. Meyers.

The doctor glanced at the paperwork in front of her. "The lab report indicates a large amount of arsenic in Ruth's system. Because of her size, her symptoms started out as a possible food poisoning, but in a few days... and I imagine she kept eating the tainted food... she became worse." Dr. Meyers continued to flip through the report. "Ruth is a drug addict, my guess is heroin because it's cheap, and she has an infection of the heart lining and valves. She also complains about severe muscle and bone pain. And with her weight, she has exacerbated her problems over the years."

Sasha asked, "Will you keep her hospitalized?"

The Doctor shook her head. "We're not required to treat drug addictions. We'll refer her to an outpatient clinic. My guess, though, is that she'll return to the camp and continue her drugs. I know it sounds sad, but that's what happens."

The officers gathered their notes and thanked the Doctor. "Now I'm hungry," Sasha said. "How about Subway?"

Alan looked once more at the photos that had been processed near Marilyn Dobbs' bookstore. If he could get even one more lead on who Gary was arguing with that day, they may get closer to an arrest. Maybe that guy knew a camera was there and how to keep out of sight. He decided to take the photos and go visit Ms. Dobbs.

When Alan walked into the bookstore, Marilyn smiled. "Detective, how can I help you?"

She was sitting on a stool behind a tall desk and appeared taller than he knew her to be. He held up a hand in greeting and then joined her at her perch. "We've looked through your CCTV and, unfortunately, the person who Officer Wagner was speaking to is off camera. I'm wondering if any of the other stores around here have surveillance."

"As far as I know, most of the cameras are inside the stores or leading out the door. You might check with the boutique across the street because she always complains about looters... usually kids, and I believe she's upgraded her system."

Alan wrote down the name of the clothes store, 'Expressions,' and then asked another question. "Has there been any street talk about what happened to my officer?"

Marilyn shook her head. "We usually cater to a sophisticated crowd who keep a low profile. They come here for a quiet break, kind of a respite from their busy lives. Very little conversation."

Alan looked at the warm, inviting open interior of the store. The welcoming environment had a variety of comfortable chairs to relax in while taking a closer look at a book that might pique a reader's curiosity. Alan wondered how many books were included on the packed cedar shelves. "I like your store. It seems like a good place to relax."

Marilyn looked appreciative. "Can I recommend a book for you?"

Alan told her about the book Maggie was reading, and Marilyn knew it immediately. She asked Alan what kind of book he preferred and when he said mysteries, she recommended a few authors.

"I'll be back later to buy a few," Alan promised.

He left the store and walked across the street. The clothes store appeared to be one that attracted younger women. The window display was filled with trendy styles including frilly dresses with tassels and graphic tees. Alan wished he had Maggie with him.

A young store clerk walked up to greet him as he entered. She was dressed in a short, cropped shirt and low waisted tight jeans. Why would someone wear that to work, Alan thought? Her make-up was dramatic, and Alan noticed her long fake eyelashes.

"Can I help you find something?"

"Is the store owner or manager around?" Alan asked.

"Let me see... " She glanced at her phone and sent a message. Not even a second later she said, "Yes, she'll be right out."

From the back room a tall, attractive lady who was probably in her late forties walked out. She had silver hair and black framed glasses. She was wearing a camel sweater and a black pleated skirt which matched nothing from the store's merchandise. "May I help you?"

Alan took out his badge and introduced himself. "I'm curious if you have CCTV footage that views activity across the street?"

The owner nodded. "We just put in a new system. Is there a problem I should be aware of?"

"Not currently. Can I see your tape from last Friday around four to six? I'm checking to see if I recognize someone."

The owner went to the counter computer and pulled up her surveillance files. "I usually erase these each week, but I guess I do have last Friday. Do you want to have a look at this?"

Alan joined her at the counter and watched the tape to see if there was a good view of Officer Wagner. Around 5:50 he noticed Wagner come onto the screen. "Stop it there." Gary had turned to look at someone and then began what appeared to be a heated conversation with another man. Alan advanced the tape until he got a good shot of that man. He then let out a long sigh. It was another police officer from his squad. "I need a copy of the tape."

By the time Alan returned to the precinct, everyone was out on duty. The officer he needed to speak with would probably leave for home when his shift ended, so Alan sent him a text, asking him to check in at the end of his day. In the meantime, Alan pulled up this officer's profile.

Joe Erickson was the older officer who had argued with Wagner about the homeless situation the morning that Alan had confronted the younger officer. Erickson had worked at the Boston precinct for fifteen years, and before that he'd been assigned to patrol in North Hampton, where he was from. He was 53, lived in the Framingham area, was divorced, and had three grown kids. Alan noticed that over the years he had been disciplined three or four times for use of excessive force. Because it had been reported that Erickson could be aggressive, he had been ordered to attend the behavioral health therapy group. It looked as though Erickson had followed the suggested coping skills they gave him. But that was two years ago.

Alan sat back in his chair and reflected on this finding. He wondered if Erickson had any peer support to help him deal with his ongoing stress management. Even experienced officers don't remain immune from the ongoing emotional and mental stress of being exposed to repeated danger. Over the years, Alan questioned if the training officers received enough support and professional resources to help them maintain their health. Several law organizations struggled to understand how stressful and traumatic the job could be and cut off resources that were sometimes urgently needed.

At 5:30 Officer Erickson knocked on Alan's office door. "Come in, and please close the door."

Erickson raised his eyebrows with concern and then moved to close the door. "You needed to talk with me, sir?"

Alan indicated that Erickson should sit. "I want to show you a tape recording I got from a store near the Market." Alan turned his computer around so Erickson could view the image of him arguing with Officer Wagner.

Visibly stunned, Erickson shook his head over and over and then said, "I know this looks bad, but we were just having a discussion about department policies."

"What policies?"

"Wagner made a crack about only using force on certain citizens and I took offense. After work I followed him to talk it out. He had some racist attitudes that kept popping up and I was finally sick of it."

"Give me an example."

"It was the language he used, sir, that annoyed me. He made negative comments about Black people, women, and LGBTQ folks... especially lesbians."

"I remember you were arguing about the homeless with Officer Wagner. You seemed upset. What was that about?"

"He was going on about people who were homeless... you probably heard that when you walked in. We were all kind of upset with his attitude."

Alan wondered if he was protecting himself or someone else, which was typical of the rapport on the force. "So, tell me how your conversation with Officer Wagner went that day on the tape."

"I caught up with him and asked him how he got such racist ideas... he turned on me and started arguing about how he had a Christian upbringing and knew there was only a right way and wrong way. I guess I was surprised that his past was so conservative... so I just backed off. Our whole discussion probably took two minutes."

"Do you know where he was headed?"

"No, sir... not a clue. Does this have something to do with where he was found?"

"We're just gathering information. Do you know of anyone else who was riled by Wagner's attitude?"

"I don't know. We all just do our own shifts and hope not to be partnered with someone who's too aggressive."

"You've had your share of discipline, I see." Alan referred to the folder on his desk.

"Yes, I have. I check in with a sponsor on a regular basis." Erickson looked Alan in the eyes and tried to show a certain amount of confidence.

"Thank you. That will be all." Alan appreciated the officer's honesty and believed he was only trying to converse with the younger officer on the tape. But why did he have to confront Wagner again... on the street?

Officer Erickson was worried. He had planned to stay outside the line of investigation. He had two more years and then he could take early retirement. He didn't want to antagonize Wagner that day, but the racism he spouted was finally getting to him.

The homeless man was a big guy... over 6'4" ... and probably weighed around 280 pounds. He claimed to never play football, but the volunteer who was talking with him wondered if he had been recruited anyway. Sometimes memories from teen years were difficult to recover. The guy's name was Mac, and he had the habit of always speaking in the plural first-person "we."

"We went out last night to find a place to sleep and were attacked!" He took off his knit cap and rubbed his bald head. "We barely got away. I need some help!" Mac always complained that someone was following him or trying to hurt him. He was a nuisance, but because of his size, the volunteer didn't want to provoke him. Lost in thought, Mac sat down on the cold concrete to try and catch his breath. When he got excited by talking too much, he felt exhausted.

"Okay, Mac, I'll try to find out who's bothering you. Where did you sleep last night?"

*Mac stopped breathing for a second to try and remember.
"Oh… yeah… we slept under the bridge with the guys."*

"Weren't you cold? It was freezing last night!"

*Mac unbuttoned his coat and then unzipped another coat.
"We have three coats on so we're okay." His grin displayed his
rotting teeth.*

*"Hey, Mac, the clinic has a free doctor on Thursdays. I
could set it up for you."*

*"We don't like doctors. They ask too many questions."
Mac was becoming uncomfortable. Struggling to his feet, he
nodded at the man and then walked away, dragging his feet.*

*The volunteer took out his notebook and wrote down
Mac's measurements. It would take a lot to take down this guy.*

FRIDAY, JANUARY 31ST

Enrique was waiting for Alan to arrive at the precinct. It had been a week since Wagner's murder, and they hadn't made much progress. There were no clues at the crime scene and although a few witnesses had been interviewed, no one claimed to have seen anything. Whoever committed this crime was very clever... or Officer Wagner had just been at the wrong place and time... or he might have witnessed something and was killed as a result. Because he was out of uniform, his identity was not known. And because he wasn't robbed, it might indicate that the suspects panicked when a train came and ran quickly away from the scene.

Alan walked into his office to see Enrique sitting by his desk and staring at the incident board. On it was a photo of Wagner and the crime scene. Listed were his parents, sisters, apartment manager and someone named Zoe. Hearing Alan's approach, Enrique asked, "Who's Zoe?"

"She's a friend of Wagner's. She came in yesterday and worried that her father was involved with the crime." Alan related all he knew of the conversation and that he was going to the restaurant in a few hours. He then told Enrique about his talk with Officer Erickson.

"Well, that's a surprise." Enrique claimed. "Do you think he had anything to do with the murder?"

Alan looked sideways out the window and then back at his partner. "I'm not sure. Let's keep that in mind while we deal with both investigations."

Enrique brought out the computer analysis from Wagner's emails and texts again. It looked like a typical group of mailings and several texts from Zoe. It appeared that the relationship was progressing slowly, as she had stated.

"What about a second phone? Anything?" Alan asked.

"Not yet. He may have used a different name, although I don't know why all the secrecy."

Alan remembered the photos he had taken of the crowd at the time of the murder. He brought these up on his computer and printed them. "Let's look closer at these individuals. Maybe someone stuck around to see if they got away with this crime."

"I could run these through face ID and see if we have anyone on file."

Alan agreed and then looked at his watch. He wanted to get to the restaurant to talk with Zoe's father before the lunch time crowd. But first, he needed to see what Connie and Sasha were investigating today.

The officers had just finished writing their reports from the previous day. When they entered Alan's office, they already had their heavy coats with them because they planned to be out on the street again.

"What are you following today?" Alan asked them.

"We're going to look for Trevor again and see if he can tell us more about who's been sick. We need to find out how the poison is distributed. Dr. Meyers said it could be anything... even bread... to disguise the taste."

"Okay, that sounds good. How about the kitchen crew

at the shelter? Have they experienced any illness?"

Connie wrote this in her notebook. "We're planning on talking with them. Deacon Martin knows them personally and can introduce us."

Alan nodded and wished them success. He knew this wasn't an easy assignment because there were so many variables involved. But why was someone poisoning such a poor and helpless group of people?

Alan arrived at the Singh restaurant at 11:00. The Cambridge traffic was already backed up because of the frozen streets, and it took some time for him to find a decent parking spot. He paid for an hour and hoped the meeting would be over quickly. When he entered the restaurant, the wonderful smell of roasting meats and vegetables made him hungry. He loved Indian food, but always forgot to think of it when he was looking for some place to eat. An older Indian gentleman saw him and motioned him to a table.

Alan remained standing and walked over to the man to show him his badge. "Are you Mr. Singh?"

The man looked frightened and nodded his head.

"Can I have a minute to talk with you?"

"Is it about my family? Is everyone okay?"

Alan smiled slightly and reassured the man that his family was fine. "This is about a customer." Taking out a photo of Gary Wagner, Alan asked, "Perhaps you've heard that one of my officers has been killed recently. I understand he ate meals here on a regular basis."

Mr. Singh looked at the photo and nodded. "Yes... yes, he did eat here. I recognize him."

"Can you tell me if he was ever with someone or if you

overheard a conversation that made you worry." Alan looked around the small restaurant and realized that people could easily eavesdrop on other customers at a nearby table. He remembered that Wagner had this habit of listening in on other conversations.

"No, Detective, I wasn't aware of anyone with him." Alan knew the man would never give away his daughter's identity.

"Was he here last Friday at any time?"

"I couldn't tell you. We are always very busy."

"Were you here last Friday?"

Mr. Singh looked speechless. He finally mumbled, "I was not here."

"Where were you on such a busy day?"

Again, Mr. Singh looked aghast. "Why do you want to know where I was? I have nothing to do with what happened to this officer."

Alan informed him that they were following all leads. When the man wouldn't say where he had been, Alan didn't pursue it. He would keep this in mind and have someone ask around about him.

When he left the restaurant, it was already filling up with customers. Alan knew he had upset the man and wondered what he was hiding. Maybe he had a financial worry, or a meeting with someone about a personal issue. This was one other thing Alan hated about investigations, causing a person to feel their lives were being scrutinized.

When Alan left the restaurant, he saw five tents bordering a vacant lot that had been fenced to keep them out. He stopped to observe the activity and noticed a family of four huddled by a stove. He wanted to go and see what he could do to help them, but then considered his position. If you're homeless you already felt low... your self-esteem was low... your mood was low. What could he offer them? There had to be more support for people who were already at risk of being criminalized for being homeless. Alan noticed a small convenience store a block away. He went inside and bought whatever food and drink he thought would help the homeless family. After paying for it, he asked the store manager to send the food over to the tent.

Connie and Sasha met Deacon Martin at the shelter an hour after lunch had been served. They had tried to locate Trevor, but after searching throughout several camps, he was nowhere to be found. The kitchen crew was just packing up when the officers approached.

"Corinne and Lola, these two officers would like to speak with you if you have the time." Levi looked at both older women with fondness. "It's about some illness that seems to be spreading in some of the camps."

Both ladies looked at him with surprise. "What do you think we know?" Corinne asked.

Connie stepped forward and introduced herself and Sasha. "We're checking in with all the clinics and food services to find out if you've heard or seen any problems with tainted food. Maybe a smell or complaints of a gritty texture."

Lola looked annoyed and spoke in a loud voice. "We've been serving food for years and we have never... ever... been accused of serving bad food!"

Connie nodded. "Of course not. We only want your help in case something bad is happening to the people you serve. Maybe you've heard that some people have been very sick, even dying, of a kind of illness. We think it might be poisoning."

Both women looked astonished. "Poison?" they said at once.

"There was a woman who was taken to Mass General with severe symptoms that turned out to be poison induced. If you hear of anyone else who is very sick, we would appreciate being notified." The officers gave the two bewildered women their cards.

Levi walked the officers out of the shelter. "How can I help?"

Sasha responded, "Let us know if you hear of any talk of poisons or anyone getting severely sick. We spoke to Trevor the other day but can't locate him right now. Do you have an idea where he might be?"

Levi shook his head. "I never know with him. He spent some years in prison and needs Suboxone to curb the pain from some injuries he incurred there. I know he favors that synthetic weed now just to get by on bad days. Anyway, sometimes he just disappears."

Connie continued probing, "He acts like some sort of helper or friend to others... kind of a director or advocate we heard."

"Oh, yeah... he's intervened in brawls and cased joints for cameras to avoid, especially at night. You might want to look over there for him." Levi pointed to a doorway across the street.

"What's there?" Connie asked.

"It leads to a place a lot of rough sleepers use when the weather's too cold for the streets. We don't say anything about it, but I hope everyone who stays there is okay... now that you mention the poisoning."

The officers found the door unlocked and went down a steep flight of stairs. They went through two doorways and down another set of stairs to a basement that looked like an underworld. Turning on their flashlights, they walked slowly through the maze of garbage and appliances that littered the floors. Several blankets and sleeping bags were curled up next to walls and appeared occupied. Connie walked over to one and leaned down to check on the person. It was a woman who looked unconscious. "Miss, can you hear me?" she said loudly. The woman raised her head and then collapsed back onto her make-shift bed.

"Go away!" she said in a whisper.

"We're here to help. Are you okay?" She could smell the reek of vomit and human waste. Sasha reached over to check the woman's pulse and noticed it was very slow. "I'm going to call for help."

By the time the EMT's arrived, the officers found several other occupants in the underground hovel. Three had signs of illness, but the medics believed it was from the draft and severe symptoms from the cold. They left supplies of food and water.

Trevor was not to be found.

Alan had to decide what to do about his interview with Mr. Singh. He didn't seem the type to kill someone, although Alan knew he never expected several criminals to act as violently as they eventually did. But Singh was hiding something and if it had something to do with Wagner's murder, he needed to find out. Enrique met him at the precinct and asked what he learned at the restaurant.

"I can't imagine that man killing anyone. But I want to review his profile and see if there's anything that might lead us to understand what he's hiding. Maybe it's nothing... will you put someone on this for me?"

"I'll take care of it," Enrique replied. "In the meantime, I ran face IDs on the people in your photos and came up with a few interesting people." Enrique took the photos out of a folder and handed them to Alan. "The big guy in the background is Trevor Reynolds, a homeless guy with a criminal record. And the woman standing next to him is Crystal Strand, and she also has a record for violence."

Alan looked at the two persons who seemed to be interested in the crime scene. "Trevor's the name of the guy Connie and Sasha were talking to when they found the woman who had been poisoned. In fact, he's the one who led them to her tent."

"Where are they now? Do you know?" Enrique was writing this down.

Just then another officer knocked on Alan's office door. "There's a call for you, Detective, from Mass General."

Alan looked surprised and answered the phone. "Detective Sharp... "

"Detective, this is Dr. Meyers from Mass General, and we have another poison victim."

Crystal Strand was 38 years old and had led a life of misfortune. She was raised by her single mother in a low rent, section 8 apartment, outside the city. Over the years, Crystal had suffered from mental health issues, and found a lack of support even from the menial jobs she held. Following the death of her mother five years ago, she lapsed into a severe depression. She tried to self-medicate and finally gave in to street drugs which landed her in jail. She eventually lost her belongings and housing which led her to the streets and struggling to find her way.

Dr. Meyers told Alan that Crystal's symptoms were poison related. She was now struggling for her life in the hospital.

SATURDAY, FEBRUARY 1ST

Alan called a morning meeting of all squad members even though it was Saturday. He wanted to be certain they all understood their roles. "We have two investigations that will take priority. First is the murder of Officer Wagner. We have interviewed family and acquaintances but have yet to find a motive. The opportunity and means may be that he was in the wrong place at the wrong time, but we won't know this until every lead is followed. I am personally leading this investigation and want all evidence sent directly to me. The second investigation is the poisoning that has been plaguing the homeless camps. We know of two women who have poison in their systems, and we also believe several illnesses may have masked actual poisonings. My understanding is that most homeless people refuse hospitalization or will be released in only seventy-two hours if they're sick. This means that they could be suffering from poison and the appropriate tests were not run. I'm sending a team out to every encampment to find out how many people have been ill or have died in the last few months. We need to find out if some kind of sociopath might be targeting this community."

Alan looked at Enrique who added a few comments. "We want you to remember the guidelines we have for approaching the public, including the homeless. Always address people with respect and use their surnames. Use diplomacy but show restraint. A good vulnerability assessment would be to ask a few questions: How long have you been homeless? Do you have family around? What kind of services do you need? Remember, it can happen to anybody. Oh… and be sure to bring a flashlight… when you enter a tent or a dark space, shine your face first so you don't startle people."

When the meeting was over, Connie and Sasha followed Alan into his office. They needed to report what they had found in the underground of the building that housed several homeless people. Crystal Strand had been staying in the building for days and was in the hospital with symptoms of poisoning, but they were still looking for Trevor Reynolds.

Sasha read from her notebook. "We don't know a lot about Crystal Strand. We found out that on top of the challenges of finding food and a safe place to sleep, most homeless women face the threat of sexual violence and cruelty. They even try and hide their identity by wearing two sweatshirts to appear more like a guy, and if they act crazy, they'll be left alone… you know… like screaming and cursing and acting wild. We heard that Crystal acted this way. She usually gravitated towards big public buildings to avoid anyone who was acting psychotic. That's probably why she was sleeping underground."

"Was she close to anyone?" Alan asked.

"Unfortunately, we heard she had been in an abusive relationship. My understanding is she's still seeing the guy because homeless women prefer the predictability of one man's violence to the unpredictability of street violence."

"I suppose we don't know who the guy is… "

"Not yet. We're trying to find a name."

Alan looked thoughtfully at both officers. "Thank you for this good work. I want you to keep searching the camps and see what you find. We need to locate Trevor Reynolds and see what he knows about the poisons and why he was at the crime scene."

"He seems like a great guy," Sasha related. "He took us straight to the sick woman's tent and said he was concerned about other people who were sick. I would be shocked to learn he was involved with a murder or a poisoning."

Enrique was on the phone to Carla when he saw Alan leave to go talk with Dr. Meyers at the hospital. He was calling Carla about locating Nick Grainger, the speaker she and Alan had heard at the town council meeting. Since Grainger was committed to finding and training volunteers, he might have knowledge of the possible poisonings from his team.

"Hello Detective Mendez. How can I help you?" Carla was always happy to help the police and expected the same in return. Her teen center always had a need for police security or advice that could help a young person make better decisions.

"Carla, Alan told me about the speaker he heard at the town meeting… Nick Grainger… and I'd like to talk with him. I want to get a list of his volunteers, and maybe what kind of services they provide."

"You know he vets all of his volunteers… "

"Of course," Enrique was quick to reply, "we're trying to find out if someone is causing harm to people in the camps, and maybe a volunteer has seen something or someone who they're concerned about."

"What kind of trouble?" Carla was on alert. She had teens in her program who were without homes and lived in shelters or on the street.

"This is confidential, but there are two women in the hospital who have been poisoned. The word is out that several people are suffering from some kind of poisoning."

"Oh, dear lord... let's hope it's just bad food. I'll text Nick's information to you. And please let me know if I can do anything on my end."

When Enrique got Carla's message, he called and left Grainger a voicemail to make an appointment. His next business was to find more background on Mr. Singh.

With the help of police tech profiles, Enrique learned that Amos Singh was born in India 48 years ago. He married at twenty-two and moved to America to help his uncle who owned a restaurant in the Boston area. He has three children, all girls, and now runs the restaurant himself. The family lives outside the city. Mr. Singh has no violations, not even a parking ticket. His affiliations included an Indian Community Center and an Indian Orthodox Church.

Enrique shook his head. This man doesn't seem to have any deviant problems. But why would his daughter think he might have hurt Wagner? Looking at his watch, Enrique decided to have lunch at the Singh restaurant and see if he might notice anything of concern.

As he was walking out of the station, his phone buzzed. "Detective Mendez? This is Nick Grainger. How can I help you?"

Enrique returned to his desk and sat. "Thank you for calling me back. I was wondering if you had time to talk with me about your volunteers. We're attempting to organize a team to go into the encampments and investigate safety issues and how we can help." That was all Enrique wanted to say now. He didn't want to alarm Grainger with talk of poisons.

"I'm free today around 2:00 if that works for you."

"I'll meet you at your office. I already have the address."

Amos Singh was watching the man who sat by the front window. He seemed out of place, maybe because he only ordered a cup of lentil soup and samosas, which were appetizers. He also kept looking around the restaurant and observing everyone who walked through the door. Amos decided it was time to approach him.

"Good afternoon, sir, how is your food?"

Enrique looked up and nodded. "It's good. I don't usually eat Indian food. Are you the owner?"

"Yes," Amos bowed. "My family has owned this restaurant for years."

"You must do a great business, being in this location."

Amos looked pleased. "Yes, it is a very good location. We work hard to feed many people."

Enrique liked this man and didn't think he had anything to do with a murder. "I'm with the police, Mr. Singh, and we are still looking for a suspect in the killing of our officer. Detective Sharp has been in here to ask a few questions, and I was wondering if you thought any more about where you were on that Friday."

Amos Singh looked around his restaurant and then sat carefully down on a chair facing Enrique. "I was at an appointment. It was with my bank. Maybe you don't know this, but almost half of food service companies are operating at a loss or just breaking even. Customers don't need to know when businesses are hurting because of the economy, and so I try and keep these things to myself."

Enrique wasn't expecting this response. He nodded and then stood up to shake Mr. Singh's hand. "I hope everything turns out okay, sir."

At 2:00, Enrique was in Nick Grainger's office. It was sparse. Located in an old building in the Back Bay, the space was not more than twelve feet by twelve feet and included a metal desk, chair, and three file cabinets. On the wall behind the desk was a city map with pins locating the several camps that the volunteers served. Nick greeted Enrique and offered a folding chair.

"How can I help?" The sincerity in his expression was noticeable and Enrique felt he could relax.

"I appreciate all you do for the homeless community. I'd like to know even more. I'm wondering how many volunteers you have."

"Right now, there are thirty-five regular volunteers who are scheduled every week. Fifty more are trained but only show up a couple times a month or even once a year."

"Can you describe the training you give them?"

"We have ongoing monthly training that concentrates on different problems that need our attention. We provide garbage removal, hygiene access, resource referral and even help to remove and relocate camps that pose a high risk to health and safety. While we're doing these clean-up duties, we engage in conversation with people and try and find out what they need to survive. Right now, it's blankets, warm jackets, socks, propane for heat... we have access to these things from public donations and try to provide as much as we can. We are humanitarians, Detective, and train our volunteers to use empathy and innovation to minimize the impact of being homeless."

"Have you heard about an illness that has been running through the camps lately? Severe stomach cramps... muscle aches... vomiting?"

"Yes. It's been alarming. I worry that my volunteers will get ill. Should we be concerned?"

"At this point, we're only aware of an illness. I would like the names of your regular volunteers so I can check in with them and see if they've heard anything about this."

"Of course, Detective. Let me get you the list. But I want you to know that I will be emailing my people and alerting them of your call."

"That's fine. Please tell them it's only a formality. And another reason is that our precinct is making a concerted effort to be more accessible to those on the street. We want to change the image we have and reach out more."

Enrique watched the man search through one of the files. He wondered how old he was and how long he would keep this position or move on politically. Grainger obviously understood the complex network of factors that led individuals to live in encampments and he knew how to respond effectively and empathetically. Hopefully, the volunteers were just as dedicated.

Alan spent the afternoon talking with Dr. Meyers. She was certain that Crystal Strand had been poisoned and wasn't sure she would make it. She was still in ICU fighting for her life.

"What's going on, Detective? It looks like arsenic poison, but we'll know for sure later today. I'm worried that more people will become ill."

"I've sent my teams to search through the camps and look for leads. Unfortunately, this is a crime you can easily get away with because the symptoms don't always occur immediately."

"True... but someone must buy the poison. Can you locate distributors of this kind of product?"

"We're only beginning our investigation. Unfortunately, arsenic can be found in rat poison or even some household products. Restrictions have been made on these products, but anyone can order anything online these days."

Dr. Meyers looked concerned. "I've alerted my staff to this, and they are watching for any case that comes through with the symptoms. I'll let you know if something comes up."

On his way back to the precinct, Alan noticed a low-income housing building that was next to the hospital with a For Rent sign hanging out front. He found the entrance door unlocked and decided to see if there was a manager available. Walking down the dark hallway, he noticed a door that was slightly open and almost hanging from rusted hinges. He was immediately overtaken by a stench coming from the room that stunk like rotted food or worse. Entering what looked like a studio apartment, Alan thought it wasn't more than a prison cell. The floor was concrete and stained with spilled drink or maybe urine. The only narrow window was barred and covered with grime. There was a filthy unmade bed up against a bare wall with a disgustingly dirty blanket and pillow lying next to it on the floor. Alan couldn't imagine what the bathroom looked like and didn't attempt to find out. In one corner was a small table with papers strewn in a pile. He walked over to look at the mail and saw eviction notices. Who would want to live here anyway? Does the city really think this is good enough? The decision to live back on the street would be a better option than existing in such a desolate space. At least on the street a person had friends and a community.

Alan was disgusted and walked away but made a note to call the city to have the place boarded up. It was unsafe and unacceptable as qualifying for housing.

The volunteer noticed the woman sitting on the street corner with bandages wrapped around her fingers. Was it injuries or the beginning of frostbite? As he approached, he knew this was another useless human being. The woman turned away from the approaching stranger. She stared at her hands and then tried to hide them beneath her coat. "Go away! I'm doing just fine!" Her voice was raised, and she looked annoyed. "I don't need help from anyone!"

Her fingers were bleeding from digging through the garbage near the restaurant on 5th Ave. Sometimes people threw away wrapped food and she knew that Saturday nights were the best time to forage. But all she located were sharp cans with razor like edges, and before she knew it, her fingers were cut. Two fingers looked to be infected after she had tried to clean them with the old soap in the filthy bathroom that all the homeless people used. Her fingers ached. Looking at the man walking away, she saw he had left her a loaf of bread. It looked fresh.

SUNDAY, FEBRUARY 2ND

The precinct was always quiet on Sundays. Alan arrived in the late morning, and there were only a few officers managing the phones. They waved at the detective and weren't surprised to see him. To most officers, it seemed that Detective Sharp lived at the station.

Walking into his office and seeing the pile of folders on his desk, Alan thought it was time to get organized. Maybe he would find something important that would move these cases along. He waded through the top folders and realized they had nothing to do with his investigations. Several files fell to the floor and when he tried to rearrange things his frustration grew. As he leaned over to pick up the mess, his phone rang. Without looking at the caller, he answered a little out of breath. "Detective Sharp here... "

"Detective... this is Henry Wagner. I was wondering if you had any news about who killed my son."

Alan had been remiss not calling the Wagner's for a few days. Of course, they were hoping that a killer had been caught and would be punished. "Thank you for calling, Mr. Wagner, I wish I could tell you more. This is a priority for us, and we continue to interview people. By the way, I'm wondering if you've heard from a friend of Gary's... Zoe Singh."

"Yes, we did. And I doubt my son had any relationship with her. They probably knew each other as acquaintances."

"Why do you say that, sir?"

"We never heard of this girl before and I think he would have mentioned her. Gary had friends, of course, and we appreciated the note she sent."

"I did speak with Zoe... she said Gary was a very good friend." Alan decided to give as little information as possible. He didn't want Henry to overreact to the idea that Gary and Zoe might have been a couple.

Henry seemed to dismiss that idea. "Well... I wish you would find the person who did this! We want answers... even though it will never give us our son back."

Alan understood and promised to call with updates.

Alan's phone rang again. It was Mass General. "Detective, we have another poisoning." Dr. Meyers sounded upset.

Alan believed they were now looking for someone who was callous and probably morally depraved. These criminals committed violent and horrible crimes. They were psychopaths who showed no empathy; felt no remorse. They lied without feeling any guilt or without any moral conscience. If caught, they blamed others or made excuses.

Yet, Alan knew they could also be very charming. So charming that people accepted the cruel gossip and biting remarks they made even when it caused embarrassment. Psychopaths had trouble with relationships anyway because they never followed the rules... they're oddly detached.

Alan knew there was no cure. They had to find this person and stop them.

Ethan West had been easily bored as a teenager. He was always on the lookout for devious exploits and was not fazed when caught. In school he was called out for what they called conduct disorder... meaning he liked to get into fights. He didn't care. When his parents met with the school officials, his inappropriate comments and profanity led to suspensions and finally to boarding school. He loved it.

Three years away from his parental discipline and rules, Ethan learned how to devise detailed plans to con and exploit generous people. He became the master of deception and found that distorting the truth worked when he was friendly and helpful. He practiced this with his teachers and became one of their favorites. They didn't realize he was the one spreading nasty rumors about their families, stealing valuables from the youngest boarders, and getting others to steal for him. He had a reckless disregard for others' safety and encouraged students to lie and steal. But because of his charisma, he became a leader.

Ethan loved math and science. He learned how to manipulate accounts and mix chemicals. He knew that one day this would come in handy. By the time he graduated, he had notebooks filled with clever ideas of how to gain control, even if it meant harm. His interests led him to the school of nursing, where he learned more about chemicals and what effect they had on people. He had a plan. And now things were going exactly as he hoped they would.

Ethan was still wearing his scrubs from work as he sat in the conference room of the old building listening to Nick

Grainger give his monthly training for the volunteers. These meetings were mandatory for the regulars who spent more hours out on the streets doing outreach. Today Ethan noticed another man standing to the side of the room and wondered who he could be.

Enrique looked carefully around the room and noticed that the volunteers appeared to be from all walks of life, and he was impressed they showed up on a Sunday morning. Nick Grainger had decided it was time to let the group know more about the illnesses that had surfaced in the camps and asked Enrique to speak, but to keep the information as brief as possible so as not to cause alarm.

When it was time for Enrique to speak, he began by thanking the volunteers for their dedication to people who were in need. He noted that the precinct wanted to work with this organization to promote goodwill and sign up to help. He then mentioned that the camps had been suffering illnesses that led to hospitalizations, and he asked if anyone knew about this. Ethan raised his hand.

"Officer, I work in a clinic and there has been a lot of illness on the streets. Can you describe the symptoms?"

Enrique appreciated the question, especially coming from a medical person. "Acute gastritis, irritation of the internal organs... vomiting... "

"So, do the police think this is some kind of intestinal virus? Is it your job to investigate something as common as a virus?" Ethan chuckled and looked around for a similar response. A few people nodded, but the rest of the room was silent.

"Are you a doctor?" Enrique inquired.

"No... a nurse. We see several street people at the clinic

and are more than aware of their problems."

Enrique nodded. "We would appreciate knowing if you see anyone with the severe symptoms I just identified."

Nick took over the rest of the meeting and reminded everyone to sign in their volunteer hours so they can continue to receive the grant money that keeps the organization going. When the room cleared out, Enrique asked Nick about the guy who asked about the symptoms.

"Oh, that's Ethan West. He's been with us for a year and is well liked. He goes out even in this cold weather and checks on the folks on the street. I keep reminding him to sign in his hours because I know he contributes more than anyone."

Enrique wrote down Ethan's name. He might want to talk with him again.

Alan reviewed the monthly police assignments to find out who had partnered with Gary Wagner on patrol. If he did struggle socially, it would probably show up in some unacceptable behavior, even unintentionally. His relationships with colleagues might have been on a superficial level, but one of the officers could have learned more. Alan wrote a list of names.

He then looked at the incident board and saw the list of questions he needed to answer. Why was Wagner in the subway tunnel? What did he do after work or with his free time? A hobby? A gym? What did he spend his money on? Alan decided he would call the police academy again and get the names of the officers who graduated with him. He was about to pick up his phone when he heard his name called.

"Hey, Alan... you're still here?" Enrique called out from the squad room. "I just got back from the training session with Nick Grainger."

"Come and tell me about it." Alan yelled out.

Enrique walked into the office and hesitated. "Have you had lunch?"

"No… you?"

"Let's see if Elizabeth is working?" Enrique had her delivery number and made the call to bring some food, a salad order for Alan, and turkey sub for him. That done, he sat in the folding chair beside Alan's desk and asked, "What's up?"

"First, tell me about the meeting."

"It was a typical volunteer meeting. I was impressed with the sophistication of the group… young and old. One guy was still in scrubs from work at a clinic and seemed interested in my explanation of the symptoms in the homeless camps. He said they had seen a lot of illness… in fact, he called it some kind of virus."

Alan thought for a moment. "Well, it's not that. I spoke with Dr. Meyers this morning and the man they found on the street was definitely poisoned. He may not make it."

"How about the lady in the ICU?"

"She has a severe infection on her hands that they're treating along with the poison. So, it's day by day."

"Can we speak with her?

"Maybe tomorrow. I'm getting worried that there's a psychopath out there who wants to do real damage to this community. If that's the case, how does he, or she, choose the victims? What do they have in common?"

"Good question. Let me follow up on that. I'll try to talk with the people in the hospital first thing in the morning. What about the Wagner case? Any leads?"

Alan told him about calling the academy and asking for names. "He must have been friends with someone there. I'm also going to talk with a few of the guys he patrolled with and see if they can think of anything. This guy is becoming a mystery."

Just then a familiar voice was heard at the office door. "What are you guys doing working today?"

Elizabeth smiled and held up two bags of food. "You're lucky, I was in the area and could grab your orders." She walked in the room and cleared a space on Alan's messy desk. "I won't say anything about this mess, Alan, but maybe an extra file cabinet would help."

Alan smirked and then smiled. "Good suggestion. How's your day going?"

"It's freezing out there today! I think I'll go home and watch my shows."

Enrique laughed. "I wish I had such a cushy job."

Elizabeth responded quickly, "We're hiring, I could put in a good word."

The men were still laughing when she left the room. As they ate the food, they made lists of what they wanted to accomplish in the next few days. Enrique was sticking with the homeless investigation and Alan would concentrate on Wagner's murder. Things were moving too slowly.

Alan stayed at the station to work on reports because he had dinner plans with Sam and Abbie at a little Italian restaurant nearby. At 5:30 they met at the entrance, shaking the newly fallen snow off their jackets. After ordering a bottle of red wine, Alan relaxed and asked, "What have you two been up to this weekend?"

The young couple spoke of basketball and a movie they

had seen, and Alan sat back and enjoyed their enthusiasm. If it wasn't too late when he got home, he would call Maggie.

Ethan West knew he shouldn't have said anything to that officer. Nick had informed the volunteers that the police had everyone's contact information. He better lie low... especially since two of the victims were hanging on in ICU. He might have to do something about that.

MONDAY, FEBRUARY 3RD

Before leaving home, Alan called the police academy to have the names of the officers in Wagner's graduating class emailed to him. Most classes started out with 45 to 50 recruits and maybe half graduated, mainly because it could be mentally and physically draining. Alan knew the ones who made it were dedicated and wanted it badly.

By the time he arrived at the precinct, he had a return email with twenty-five names. Next to nine names was a check that indicated a possible lead. His friend Simon Garrison had made a note that these few had the same classes and instructors at Wagner. Alan appreciated not having to call every officer.

He then looked through Wagner's assignment schedules and found the names of four officers in the precinct who had been on duty with Wagner. Because he was a recruit, he had been assigned different partners over the months to see if a good match would become obvious. Alan made appointments to meet with these four officers today.

Next, Alan called the city housing council about the unsanitary conditions of the old apartment building by the hospital he saw last week. The person he spoke to knew of the building and said it had been condemned, but that didn't keep people out. There were three floors of equally filthy rooms that had been boarded up, but people found a way to crawl in and hide or seek shelter. The person on the phone promised to send someone over to board it up again.

Alan crossed this off his list and then noticed one of the officers he needed to speak to standing outside his door. Officer Fleming was older, a seasoned officer, and Alan knew he had the respect of the squad because of his fairness and cooperation. His motto was always: 'Gather facts first and then keep your cool.'

Alan signaled for the officer to enter. "Please come in. I just have a few questions."

The officer looked concerned, wondering if he had violated some rule. "Yes, sir. Did I do something you wanted to talk with me about?"

Alan chided himself for not explaining to the officers he notified that this was only a quick inquiry to help with the investigation. "No... no. Sorry. I should have mentioned it was to learn more about Officer Wagner. I understand you rode with him for a couple of months and wondered if there was anything you can remember that might help our case."

"I've thought about it, sir. I guess the only thing I wondered about was what he did after work. I asked him that and he was always suspiciously non-committal. To me, it was odd because we guys all share what we do... sports, gym, family, kids... we're like a community."

"Did anyone pursue this further?"

"Not to my knowledge. We just gave him space."

"I heard he had a side to his personality that was more smart talk and less sensitive. Do you agree?"

"Yes, I would. I think that's why we gave him space.

Maybe it was his personality, but he could put down an idea or a person with what seemed like spiteful intent."

"Did he ever lose control? Or have difficulty tolerating some rules or conditions he faced on the job?"

"You know I hate to say anything bad about another cop, but Wagner had a need for exact order and there were times I just didn't care for his inflexibility. He kind of wore me down."

"Can you give me an example?"

"Everything had to go by the book. That included how we wrote up reports, approached citizens, and even where we had meals. The guy acted like the world would end if we didn't keep to the rules."

Alan nodded and knew this went along with what he had already learned about Wagner. But if he was getting help from a therapist, he must have wanted to change some of this behavior. "I've heard similar complaints about Wagner. Officer Fleming, I have an assignment for you. Here's a list of several academy classmates of Wagner's. I want you to call each one and ask them how they got along with him. We're still looking for clues and reasons why someone would want him dead."

Officer Fleming took the list and promised to report back later in the day. Alan knew he would keep their conversation confidential.

Dr. Erik Stanton felt a personal sense of guilt for not being able to assist with the investigation of Gary's death. The doctor had been getting closer to his patient, learning more of his secrets, and understanding his deep desire to change. After reviewing his notes for the months that Gary had been in therapy, Dr. Stanton decided to call Detective Sharp and reveal some candid thoughts about his patient.

Alan was surprised when his phone rang and saw it was the doctor.

"Detective, I've reviewed my case notes on Gary Wagner, and I'm willing to make exceptions for some personal knowledge I have on him."

"I would appreciate learning anything new." Alan thought he heard an urgency in the doctor's voice.

"As you know, Gary was trying to understand the root causes of his personal addictive behavior and trying to get free from the destructive cycles. He was beginning to make plans for positive productive steps. You must realize that human behavior is context driven, and changing the circumstances often changes the behavior."

Alan interrupted, "Can you tell me what steps or changes he was attempting?"

"Yes. Gary told me he overreacted when he spoke with you at the station about the homeless situation. He felt judged by his response and then carried a grudge with him when he went to the shelter the next day. He planned to relieve his guilt by signing up to volunteer at a shelter and force himself to step outside of his need for control."

"Doctor, do you know if he did sign up?"

"Yes. The last time I spoke to him, by phone, he said he had an appointment with a person at a shelter in the city. I'm not certain which one and, unfortunately, he was killed before our next session."

"Is there anything else you can tell me?"

"I feel I'm giving more than I should, Detective. I want to

stay unconnected to your case and not involved in any way. I hope this information helps you." The doctor rang off before Alan could ask any other questions.

Enrique waited outside the woman's hospital room. She had been in ICU with little hope for recovery, and because she didn't have any ID, they listed her as a Jane Doe. He learned earlier that she seemed to rally, so Enrique was waiting for the opportunity to talk with her. A floor nurse saw him and nodded as she walked out of the woman's room and indicated he had about five minutes.

The woman was hooked to several systems and appeared to be asleep. Enrique leaned close to the woman and said in a low voice, "Hello, can I speak with you for a minute?"

The woman's eye shot open and tried to focus on him. She had a tube in her mouth and couldn't speak clearly. Enrique knew she was scared. "You're in the hospital. It looks like you were given some tainted food or drink that caused you to have severe symptoms. Someone called an ambulance. Do you remember who that was?"

The woman closed her eyes and shook her head. "That's okay. We don't need that information now. Did someone give you food or drink that made you sick?"

The woman appeared to be thinking because her eyes looked from left to right as if reviewing what had happened. She then nodded and spoke almost incoherently, "A muhn gave me bruhad."

"Do you know who he was?"

The woman shook her head.

Enrique thanked her and let her drift off. He needed to

get the CCTV footage of the street where the woman was found. Someone had given her bread laced with something, and as far as the Doctor knew, it had poisoned her.

Alan looked at his watch and hurried out of his office. He had made plans to have a late lunch with his friend Sidney at the nearby sandwich restaurant. It was close to his precinct, but he was already ten minutes late. Sidney was waiting at a table by the window when he rushed in.

"Sorry I'm late, Sidney. I need to get the alarm working on my phone to remind me of things like lunch with friends." Alan shook Sidney's hand warmly and settled into a chair. He felt comfortable pleading forgiveness.

"That's okay, my friend. Let's order before we settle into a conversation."

Looking at the menu, both men knew they would order their usual… the corn beef on light rye and homemade coleslaw. They came here often because the service was great, and the staff was overly friendly. Once their order was taken, Sidney asked about Alan's investigation.

"Slowly, I'm afraid. Officer Wagner seems to be a mystery. I may have gotten a break earlier today when I spoke with his therapist, but I'll have to see once I follow it up."

"Anything I can help you with?" Sidney was a partner at a large law firm and didn't mind researching or discussing cases with Alan. When a paralegal at his office was found murdered over a year ago, Alan led the investigation and leaned on Sidney for information.

"You know that old building by Mass General… the low-income apartments? I went in to check on something last week and it was in horrible condition. I called the city today to get it boarded up, but I wonder how fast that will happen."

"I'll see what I can do. These things take a long time to get done... you know why... too many layers to channel through. Was anyone living there?"

"Not that I could tell. It was filthy! The other day Carla invited me to a town council meeting to listen to Nick Grainger speak about the volunteers he sends out on the streets. I can't imagine what kind of chaos these people see daily. I suppose you hear a lot about this from Carla."

Sidney nodded. "She's amazing. Working with kids who are desperately in need of care puts her in the category of saint. Where do these kids go when they have no home to return to? It breaks her heart to know that they're homeless or in shelters."

Alan looked dismayed. "Nick Grainger's trying to organize more volunteers to support the homeless. But what about building more houses? I heard if a thousand houses were built today, every year would require five hundred more to keep up with the need. What kind of system is that?"

Sidney shook his head. Being a lawyer and a Black man, he was able to step into various communities and give legal advice and assistance to people from all walks of life. Sidney offered his services pro bono to several clients while still working as a full partner at his firm. "It's just that housing and the cost of living is so damn expensive! If folks are expected to spend over forty percent of their income on rent, many of them can't keep up. And homelessness is the result."

Alan understood. They had talked about this several times and recognized the need for a better support structure through public agencies and privately funded organizations. This meant better leadership, but politicians who promised to

151

help the homeless seemed to ignore it once they got elected. The bottom line was that the homeless problem needed more than one solution because there were all different types of homelessness. It takes many forms, but one thing was true... lack of affordable housing.

Alan changed the subject. "Have you heard of an illness going around in the homeless camps?"

Sidney shook his head. "What sort of illness?"

"Severe symptoms that might mask poisoning. There are three people in the hospital with suspected arsenic poisoning. One woman might not make it... and if that's the case, it'll be an investigation for murder."

Sidney put down his sandwich and stared at Alan. "Why in the world would anyone want to hurt people who are in survival mode at best. Did you tell Carla?"

"Yes, I did. Her vulnerable community has been put on alert. We've begun to send messages to shelters and encampments to not accept food from people they don't know. It's the kind of poison that can easily be hidden, especially in strong flavors like coffee or soup."

"Will this get in the press? My thinking is that it might do two things, stop people from donating food or give this idea to criminals. You'll have to be careful."

"My thoughts exactly. Right now, we're labeling this outbreak a GI virus and asking people to let the volunteers know if they're sick. But you know how things get out... the media would love to get everyone riled up."

The men talked some more and then promised to keep in touch. Alan decided to walk back to the subway tunnel where Wagner had been killed. Walking down the subway stairs, he saw two men sitting beside the tile wall hoping for a handout. One man was wearing torn, dirty jeans and a Boston Celtic hooded sweatshirt. His long hair was tied with a cord and his eyes looked dull. The other man was more alert and had on a down jacket and winter boots. Alan approached the men and held out his badge. "Hey, fellows, can I ask you something?"

The men looked frightened. "What do you want?" asked one man abruptly.

"Are you here regularly?"

"What do 'ya mean? You gonna chase us off or arrest us for trespassing?"

Alan took out his phone and showed them the photo of the two homeless people he had seen at the crime scene. "Do you know these two?" Both men stared at the phone and shook their heads.

"The woman, whose name is Crystal Strand, is in the hospital very sick. We're trying to locate the man who's standing next to her in the photo. Have you seen him?"

The man who seemed to be in a stupor, muttered, "That's Trevor... "

The other man stood and seemed upset. "I ain't gonna help anyone find Trevor. He's a good guy and never hurt anyone... " and he stomped away.

Alan watched the man hurry through the tunnel. He wondered if he had a hiding place somewhere down the track like the guy who found Wagner. Had Wagner been following one of the homeless when he was attacked? This area was being patrolled, but maybe they needed to search other tunnels and look for suspects.

When Alan got back to the precinct, Officer Fleming was waiting for him. "Sir, I managed to talk with six of the ten people on the academy list. Three were non-committal and said they didn't really know Wagner, two refused to answer any questions, and one was very outspoken."

Alan was waiting. "What did he say?"

"It was a woman, sir. She said that Wagner needed a lot of attention. He tried to manipulate the class with long winded discourses that usually painted someone like him as a victim. He excelled in negotiating, but always spoke in an inauthentic manner... she said it was borderline narcissistic."

"I wonder if the instructors picked up on any of this." Alan said.

"Well, that's what I wonder, too. I think I'll call a couple instructors and find out what they think. If that's okay... "

"Good idea. Thank you, Officer."

Alan's phone rang. Enrique urgently reported, "Our Jane Doe just died, Alan. We've got a murder on our hands now."

TUESDAY, FEBRUARY 4TH

On impulse, Alan decided to walk to the nearby coffee shop before heading to the office. On the street corner, he noticed a man dressed in ragged clothes and loudly muttering garbled words while gyrating his arms in the air. He appeared to be in a kind of fugue state, and when Alan asked for his name, he was unable to recall his identity or even his first name. The man suddenly jumped to the side of a building when a blast of traffic noise sounded from the jammed intersection. It appeared that the chaos... automobiles, blaring horns, screeching tires... seemed to attack him as he pressed his hands to his ears to block it out. Most doctors would characterize this behavior as post-traumatic stress disorder.

Alan was aware of the man's frenzy and pointed to a coffee shop on the other side of the street. "Sir, can I buy you breakfast?"

The man perked up and nodded and began walking with his ears still covered. As they secured a table by the window, Alan ordered a full breakfast for the man and coffee for himself.

Trying to put the man at ease and maybe prick his memory, Alan asked, "Where have you been this morning?"

The man looked puzzled, then seemed to remember

something. "I had to find somebody." He took a big gulp of water and seemed to be fighting for control. "He stole my things."

"What did the man steal?"

That started the man off on a kind of tangent. "My things are all gone... he took them... they were mine... when I woke up everything was gone... "

Alan knew there were no boundaries these days for homeless people. Because of the lack of order and trust, an incredible amount of theft was done by homeless people stealing from each other. The reality was, when you're broke, you steal from everyone to survive. As a result, frustration was growing on the street and tension was building.

When the food arrived, the starving man hunkered protectively over his plate, so no one would grab it. He had learned to guard his possessions, and food was one of the most valuable stolen items, along with cigarettes and batteries. You couldn't blame him for feeling cautious.

As soon as the food was gone, the man looked around, as if to escape. Alan quickly motioned to the waitress to bring more coffee to keep the man from running off. He then took out his notebook and pen and said, "Let me write down what was stolen so I can make a report."

The man studied him and tapped his fingers rapidly on the table. "I had a water bottle... and food in my backpack. They took it all." He shook his head and leaned over the table to speak quietly. "I keep the food in a plastic container, so it'll be fresh... now that's gone."

Alan considered this. "I can get you another backpack and some water and food. Did you have any personal items in your possession?"

"Just my pocket knife. It belonged to my dad... now it's gone." Tears were forming in the corners of the man's eyes.

"Do you have any idea who took your things?"

"I think it's that guy in the tent who lives on Mass Ave. He steals from everyone!" At this point the man raised his voice.

Alan motioned for the man to settle down. He then pulled out his phone and showed him the photo of Trevor Reynolds. "Do you know this guy?"

The man stared at the picture and then back to Alan. "Why? What's he done?"

"I just want to speak with him." Alan said calmly.

The man took another gulp of coffee. "If I tell you, can I go?"

Alan nodded and repeated, "I only want to talk with him."

"He's staying at the camp by the hospital. His friend Crystal... she's at Mass General, and he tries to get in to see her when no one's looking." The man stood and mumbled thanks to Alan and hurried out the door.

Enrique was waiting when Alan arrived at the precinct. "Another poison victim just got diagnosed. This time it's a teen." Enrique referred to his notes and said the teen lived in a hotel with some other kids and did odd jobs when he found work. "Dr. Meyers reported that his symptoms were less severe because of his age, but he was still very sick. What do you want to do?"

"Let's go find out what he's eaten. Do you have the address of the hotel?"

Enrique nodded and offered to drive. On the way, they discussed what Alan learned about Trevor Reynolds and what

Officer Fleming had reported about Wagner. "It seems we're going in circles with both investigations." Enrique admitted. "We need to catch a break. Why poisoning? Why Wagner?"

The hotel where the teens were staying was a cheap two floor building with twenty-four units. No one came to the front desk when the officers rang the bell. They had read the ratings for this run-down hotel and knew there were complaints about the lack of hot water pressure and even water damage in bathrooms. Maybe the manager was out fixing the problems. They decided to go have a look.

A large woman stood in the doorway of one room on the ground floor and watched the men approach. She looked back through the open door of the unit.

"What do you think they want?" she asked her bulky husband who was perched on the bed eating chips.

"Who?"

"Some guys who just came out of the lobby."

What do they look like?"

"Like cops."

"Don't talk to them. Come back inside." The man brushed the crumbs from his large belly and burped from the soda he just gulped. "Are the kids in school?"

"Where else would they be?" The woman rolled her eyes, knowing that he never cared where the kids were. To him, they were just mouths to feed.

"Close the door. Don't let them in." The man reached for the remote and turned the sound up, so he didn't have to deal with anything. Police were always snooping around the hotel trying to disturb whatever shelter they had, even if it was only for the month.

Alan approached the heavy-set woman and took his

badge out. He smiled to indicate he was there not to evict them, but to ask some questions. "I'm Detective Alan Sharp and I'm looking for someone. Do you have a minute?"

The woman nodded and folded her arms around her wide chest. "Who?"

"A teen who lives around here was very sick and taken to Mass General. We need to know where he lives. His name is Jake."

"Never heard of him." The woman coughed loudly without covering her mouth. Alan stared at her and held his ground.

"We're also looking for a man named Trevor Reynolds."

"What do you want me to do about it?" The woman stared at Alan with contempt. "I have enough to do without helping the police look for suspects. Maybe you could help me look for a job!"

Alan nodded. He was frequently blamed for problems not handled by the organizations who promised to send supplies, housing, food, or anything that will help people get off the street.

"What kind of a job do you need?"

"I used to work in the schools. When the cuts came, I lost hours and couldn't pay for daycare for my kids. So here we are... living in a hotel since I couldn't pay my rent either. Do you think I'm happy about this?" The woman shifted her weight and leaned heavily against the hotel door. "I have three kids and a husband, and we live in this small room with all our belongings! Every day we're scared something will happen to make us leave... and we'll be on the street. So... no... officer... I don't really care about your suspect."

Alan nodded and walked back to Enrique. "No luck

there. We'll have to knock on a few doors to find the right room with the teens."

"Why would teens live here? Don't they need a guardian?"

"This hotel kind of living is usually due to emergencies when teens can't be placed in foster care. It's only temporary and they have a social worker who checks in. It's never a good solution, and it stands to reason that they're at-risk kids who have behavior and medical problems."

Alan looked at the littered walkway. "Let's hope we have the right address."

After knocking on several doors and getting no response, an upstairs door opened, and a young teen walked out. Alan and Enrique were at the end of the corridor and called out for him to stop for a minute. Frightened, the teen searched for his keys to get back into the room. By the time he had opened the door, Enrique had rushed to block it from closing. Inside were two other teens lying on the beds that looked as hard as plywood with blankets as cushions. There were flies circling the two cheap lamps that were dimly lit. Clothes were piled on the floor because there were no dressers and it looked like the bathroom door was off kilter. The room smelled of sweat and spoiled food.

Alan took out his badge and looked for a reaction from the teens. Two appeared stunned and the other one seemed to ignore the officer's presence. "Can I buy you guys lunch?"

All eyes were on Alan now. "How about the Burger King across the street?"

The teens stood and looked at each other for approval. Alan could imagine they were hungry... what kid wasn't... and he wanted to get them out of the smelly room. One by one they walked out the door.

After ordering burgers, fries and milkshakes, Alan asked the boys their names. Reluctantly, the boy who appeared the oldest, Brody, began to speak. "We're staying at the hotel because they can't find us another place. Our case worker knows about us… she comes over to check that we're okay."

"Can you give me her name?"

They looked at each other and agreed it would be okay. Brody spoke up. "It's Lucy Newland. She's with CPS."

Enrique wrote that down and then asked, "How long have you been staying in the hotel?"

Taking the lead again, Brody continued to answer the questions. "About six weeks. There's another kid who lives here, too, but he got sick."

"That's the reason we're here," Enrique said, "we think he ate something that made him sick. Did he say anything about this?"

The boys looked at each other and then took big gulps from their shakes. They agreed that they didn't know anything about what their friend ate. The youngest boy quietly said, "We get food stamps and buy things from the store down the street. We have an ice chest for cold things, and sometimes we go to the shelter for meals."

Alan felt sorry for these kids. They couldn't be older than sixteen or seventeen and had to take care of themselves. Where was their family? He wanted to warn them to be careful. "There's an illness going around the camps right now that's causing severe reactions. We believe it's from tainted food and your friend has symptoms of having eaten some of that food. We don't know where or who is giving this out, whether it's intentional or not, but we want to warn you not to take any food from someone you don't know."

The boys looked worried. Brody seemed the most alarmed. "Do you mean like poison? Someone is giving out food with poison in it?"

Enrique put his hand up to caution them. "We aren't sure. But we're following up on some cases of interest. Hopefully, your friend will be okay... from what we know he's recovering. But you boys be careful."

When they left the fast-food restaurant, Alan bought the boys more burgers and fries for later. As he watched the three teens walk back to the hotel, he made a call to Carla. She would take over from here.

Ethan West was upset. That kid wasn't supposed to get the stuff he'd dropped off for the old guy. What were the chances that the kid was walking by when the crazy guy stopped him and shoved the warm roll into his hand. Ethan followed the kid and tried to snatch the roll away, but the kid took off. He found out hours later that some teen was in ICU with acute stomach pain. It had to be that kid.

Ethan knew he had to be careful. It had been easy for him to enter Mass General the night before and finish the job on the lady in ICU. The shot he added to her IV would never be discovered. He thought he had already given her enough chemicals to end her misery, but when she made it through the first day, he had to act. He worried that she would be able to identify him.

Ethan's motivation for killing had nothing to do with revenge, mental illness, or addiction. It was all about the thrill of committing a crime and getting away with it. Targeting the homeless population fell onto his radar when he heard his fellow classmates at nursing school complain about being abused by homeless people who were strung out on drugs when they arrived at the hospital. They had bruises and cuts from violent attacks and worried about infections. Ethan listened to the complaints and then decided to begin his own attacks. His idea to use poison to rid the streets of sick and confused street people was easy. He was a master with chemicals. And... after all... wasn't he doing the city a favor?

Lieutenant Johnson met the detectives at the precinct when they returned. "We need to talk. I've got an FBI profiler coming in tomorrow morning to help investigate the murder of our officer. We're moving too slowly and need to find the killer ASAP." He walked out the door.

Alan and Enrique knew this was a possibility. Police murders were always a federal concern and specialists were usually called. "Let's get here early tomorrow," Alan advised his partner. "Things will be hopping in the morning."

Alan opened his townhouse door and found Harry running up to greet him. The dog had been staying with Sam for a week, and now it was Alan's turn to have company. He grabbed the dog leash, and they started out for a walk to the park. Harry was aging like his master and took his time to enjoy the cold air. Snow was still on the ground and was in the forecast again which was not a surprise for the city of Boston.

When they had had a good amount of exercise and returned home, Alan made himself a quick meal and decided to call Maggie. It wasn't too late, he hoped. "Hello! Are you free to talk for a few minutes!"

"Alan! I've been thinking about calling you! How is your investigation going?"

Alan liked the fact that Maggie was always interested in

his line of work. A lot of people preferred to avoid hearing bad news, especially when it came to murders or other tragic subjects. Maggie only listened for the effects it had on Alan and remained sympathetic to his feelings of frustration especially when a case moved slowly. "I wish I could tell you that we caught the person who did this, but we're not there yet. How are you doing?"

Because Alan sounded a bit discouraged, Maggie thought he might want to talk more about his case. "Do you have any suspects yet?"

Alan, although reluctant, replied, "No, and my lieutenant has called in a profiler to help us. Someone from the FBI."

"What will they do? Don't you already have an idea of who this criminal might be?"

"Well, yes and no. When it comes to an investigation of one of our team, we often call experts in for help. Profiling has gotten more accurate throughout the years, and, truthfully, I'm not a great profiler. I tend to accept what's written by an expert or professional and then take it from there."

"Is this psychological profiling?"

"That and scientific analysis. If you think about it, profiles are mainly based on opinions or decisions made by a subjective profiler, so we work closely to stay objective. Does that make sense?"

Maggie smiled into the phone. "I can't imagine all you have to deal with to solve a case, Alan. When will the profiler be at the precinct?"

"Tomorrow morning."

WEDNESDAY, FEBRUARY 5TH

Television profilers are usually cast as young brainy millennials who wear odd hair styles and baggy clothes. Either that or a fast-talking whiz kid who never sits for long, always pacing and talking. Agent Lee Ra Ha was not that type. Korean born Lee, as he would prefer to be called, wore a tailor-made black suit, a stark white shirt, and a light blue tie. His hair was perfectly trimmed, and his shoes were shined. He looked to be in his mid twenties, although that was a guess. Holding out his hand to Alan, he introduced himself. "Detective, I am honored to meet you." He then reached for Enrique's hand and bowed slightly as they shook.

Although Alan was surprised to see such a young person with credentials as a profiler, he got right to the point. "Where do we start?"

Looking around the small office, Lee had a thought. "Is there a conference room we might use? Perhaps with a white board to keep track of our thoughts?"

Alan and Enrique led Lee to the largest room available. The stained-glass window overlooking the market made the room less dull because the table and chairs were old school, uncomfortable looking, and brown. The solid brick wall in the front of the room held a map of the Boston area and a bulletin board in the back was filled with posters and announcements.

Lee took this in and looked for the white board. Enrique spoke up, "We're bringing a board in right now."

Once the men were seated at the table, Lee began his inquiries. "What I want to do is try to identify the suspect's mental, emotional, and personality characteristics based on things done or left undone at the crime scene. I need to interpret the offender's behavior during and interactions between the crime." He stopped and looked at the Detectives.

Alan spoke up, "And then you compare that to similar crimes?"

"Yes. I will analyze and compare similar crimes through an in-depth analysis, and then look at the victim's background and activities for possible motives and connections. In this way, I'll be developing descriptions of possible offenders."

Enrique looked suspicious. "What if it's just one perp? Some guy who was just passing through the city?"

Lee nodded. "Modus Operandi. Some guy who might have a fantasy-based behavior against cops, likes rituals, leaves a signature of some kind... I'll be looking for this."

Alan sat back a moment and then had a thought. "Most profiling assumes that behavior is primarily determined by personality not situational factors. I would assume that a planned organized crime is usually committed by a highly intelligent person, as opposed to an unplanned, disorganized one that might be by someone of low intelligence."

Lee nodded. "That is a good assumption, Detective." He then stood to face the white board, now in front of the room. "Gentlemen, I want to write down all you have learned about the victim, Officer Wagner, and his activities. Why did the offender choose him to follow and to kill?"

The next hour was spent examining the information already collected about Wagner and the crime. Lee also wanted time to study the lab report, and after lunch go to the crime scene. His obvious objective was to gather as much information as he could before considering a possible profile.

At 2:00, the three men walked at a good pace to the State Street Tunnel. The Boston weather was holding at two degrees below freezing at what the forecasters kept calling chilly. Even though it was mid-afternoon, the skies were darkened which made the streets a slick coat of ice. Alan wondered if Lee's leather shoes would cause him to slip on the cold winter sheen but had to admit he admired the young man's style. As always, Alan was comfortable with his overcoat and sensible heavy shoes.

It had been twelve days since the murder, and the crime scene had been thoroughly searched, videotaped, and analyzed. There was a patrol officer leaning on the wall by the caution signs who stood at attention when he saw Alan approach. "Detective, can I help with anything?"

Alan shook the officer's hand and introduced Agent Lee. "We'll just look around and then be on our way."

Lee held his phone close to his face and appeared to be talking into the speaker. Walking down the tunnel a way, he stopped several times to examine the tunnel walls. At one point he took a photo and cast a flashlight beam onto the wall. Curious, Alan and Enrique walked over to see what he was looking at.

"Did you see this?" Lee pointed to a hole in the wall. "I believe it's a bullet hole."

Alan looked carefully at the damaged wall and thought this might be true. He immediately called his forensic team to examine the area. How did they miss that?

When the team arrived, the three men decided to warm up at the corner coffee shop. Alan was curious about Lee and started asking questions. "What got you involved with profiling?"

Lee took a sip of his Latte and smiled. "I wanted to be a professional baseball player. I played for a couple of years and then sustained an injury that required an operation. My sports star dreams came to an end. I have a degree in psychology, criminal justice, and behavioral science, and decided on the police force. Then I was encouraged to apply to the FBI."

Enrique asked, "What kind of skills do you need to be a criminal profiler?"

Lee looked at Enrique with a note of surprise. "We have several areas of expertise. The attention to detail is very useful. Every piece of evidence provides clues, as you know, even social cues and patterns that are not obvious to most people. We are given training to analyze complex data because of the attention needed to detect small details. Communication skills are required so we can explain our theories and conclusions in a comprehensive way. And, Detective, this is most important, we must have physical stamina." Lee laughed when he said this. "We all joke about this because we have some agents who refuse to get in shape."

Later in the afternoon the two officers reviewed the case with Agent Lee. He was interested in Officer Wagner's tendencies for repetitive behaviors, need for order, difficulty tolerating uncertainty and the need to follow a strict routine. Agent Lee explained. "Obsessive compulsive individuals see the world as good or bad. They can make unreasonable and inflexible demands on themselves and others which ends in unstable relationships. As a result, the person experiences feelings of emptiness and the more control he tries to exert, the more out of control he feels. Does this sound like Officer Wagner?"

Alan nodded his head slightly. "We're learning more as we go because he'd only been assigned to the precinct for a few months. We've tried to contact his former academy instructors and classmates, but no one wants to say much of anything. The therapist he was seeing over the past months was convinced that Wagner was making progress and trying to address the problems you mentioned. And a woman who was a friend of his paints a totally different picture. She says he was concerned about others and tried to build confidence with his patrol partners. What do you think this all means?"

"First, I want to address his prejudice against the homeless population because I believe this could play a part in arriving at a profile for the killer. What is the reason that Officer Wagner had such a strong reaction to this community? If this were true, and he had no regard for anyone in terms of their personal struggle, that would also explain his relationship with his colleagues which seemed to be on a superficial level."

Lee glanced at his notes and asked, "Is there a similar case involving the homeless population in the past few months?"

Alan and Enrique looked at each other. They didn't see a connection between the poisoning they were investigating, and the murder of Officer Wagner. Enrique spoke up. "We're in the middle of an investigation within the homeless community. We believe someone is intentionally poisoning people and, in fact, one person has died from arsenic poisoning."

Alan interrupted, "There might be a connection... although it seems far-fetched... but Wagner's therapist said he was planning to sign up to volunteer with a homeless shelter. We should check and see if he did that."

Agent Lee was writing this down. "That gives me more to work on. In the meantime, I want to find out what crimes were reported in the vicinity of the murder, during the week... before and after. I'll be going over the lab reports and the witness statements. I should have something for you tomorrow."

The two Detectives were impressed. Having someone like Lee on their team, laying things out clearly and concisely, might help them find the killer.

Arsenic is a metal that looks like white powder. If ingested, it causes severe gastric distress, maybe a burning pain in your throat, probably vomiting and diarrhea. Symptoms begin as early as thirty minutes after ingesting. Depending on the dose, people can die within hours, others can take as long as twenty-four hours. This gives the poisoner time to get away, after administering the poison. Ethan West relied on this tactic. Be nowhere in sight when the death occurred.

Walking into the downtown shelter to help the kitchen crew, Ethan waved at the two women who had just completed the lunch service. His regular schedule of serving dinner began at 5:00 and he was ten minutes late. "Hey, Levi, sorry I'm late. We were swamped at the clinic." Deacon Levi nodded and smiled at the volunteer who could always be relied on. "No problem, Ethan, we're always happy to see you."

Keeping a low profile was easy in a place as busy as the shelter. Volunteer jobs included serving, washing up and walking around with coffee and water while visiting with the street people who hardly noticed his presence. Ethan despised these worthless people. They lived off his tax money and left garbage wherever they went. So far, his plan was working. Tonight, he would follow a guy who was going to be evicted from his camp and offer him the goods.

\

THURSDAY, FEBRUARY 6TH

Agent Lee had spent the greater part of the evening analyzing the information he had gathered the day before. He had spoken with Lloyd Randell and determined that the injuries caused by the murder were probably from a person over six feet and appeared to have been defensive. Officer Wagner might have been ambushed and didn't have the time to react quickly. The force the perpetrator used on him, multiple blows, and strangulation, almost appeared frantic. Agent Lee wondered if drugs could be the reason.

Police killers generally range in age between eighteen and thirty-seven and usually kill on impulse, although some kill for reasons such as cop-hating or mental health conditions. Lee knew that many suspects were often involved in drug crimes just before murdering an officer, and if that rings true, a chase could be involved. If Officer Wagner had followed a suspect into the tunnel to question some illegal activity he had observed, that could be the reason for the attack.

A gun had not been found around the vicinity of the crime scene, but the bullet found in the tunnel wall was from a Glock 45. This was a solid choice for a personal open carry or home defense gun. It could belong to anyone. If a gun had been fired, the noise of the subway would have muffled the sound unless Officer Wagner was close by, heard the shot, and was investigating a potential incident. Was Wager only following up on a lead?

So, what crimes had been reported in that vicinity that day or a few days before?

Alan had received an early morning call from the hospital. There had been another poisoning. A homeless man had been brought in during the night and rushed into surgery. He had been found convulsing and gasping for air near the State Street tunnel. Alan was told that the amount of arsenic in his system had been a large and fatal dose. He died in surgery.

By the time Alan reached the hospital, Officers Beale and Lane were already there. Sasha approached Alan with details about the victim. "Ray Robinson, age 56, moved from Detroit to Boston one year ago. Was a welder and now had a job in construction. Some say he was saving to get an apartment. I guess his camp area was going to be evicted soon." Sasha closed her notebook. "That's all we could find out. We'll keep asking around."

Alan nodded. "See if you can find the next of kin and let me know. Once again, be sure to check the CCTV cameras in the area. We need to get a warning out to the public that there's a suspect doing harm and now killing people on the street. I'll have someone write it up today." Alan left word to have Dr. Meyers call him when she got to work.

Enrique met Alan when he returned to the station. "Agent Lee would like to speak with us. Do you have a minute?"

Alan agreed and they proceeded to his office and called Lee. Ten minutes later the agent arrived and stood beside the incident board where Officer Wagner's photo and details were listed. "I have just a few things: Most police killings are impulsive and occur when officers try to question their attacker about suspicious activity or to make an arrest. The fact that Officer Wagner was out of uniform tells me that his actions were probably impulsive. From what you tell me about him, his sense of duty was strong, and we must question his internal logic and operational principles for pursuing this killer. If the officer preferred his life laid out clearly and concisely, he most likely knew the suspect and felt justified going after him. So, we need to find out two things: one—who had Officer Wagner been following in the weeks before and two—what crimes had been committed in the area where the murder took place."

Alan and Enrique agreed.

But Agent Lee wasn't finished with his analysis. "Detectives, I believe that your homeless situation, the poisonings, might have something to do with the murder." The look of surprise on the Detectives faces was acknowledged. "The reason I think this might be a possibility, is because of the similarities I have found in other cases. Beatings and strangulations often occur in encampments." There was urgency in the agent's voice. This simple fact opened startling possibilities.

Alan spoke up. "Okay... we know there are two kinds of murder, premeditated and out of passion. So, why Wagner? And why did Officer Wagner and the killer have a fight... the blows were multiple, they kept hitting... You think Wagner only tried to ward off his attacker and lost?"

Lee shook his head. "In my work, it doesn't make a difference what I believe, I'm only looking for the truth. So far, this is only speculation. I'll keep studying the witness statements, autopsy and lab reports and every scrap of paper the police have compiled about this homicide."

The Detectives were impressed and appreciative of Lee's analysis. Alan thought out loud, "It would help the investigation if we knew that the killer was a drifter... or an outsider. The important question is will he kill again?"

He then looked seriously at Agent Lee to report the latest news. "In the meantime, we've just come from the hospital and another person has been poisoned... this time it's murder."

Trevor Reynolds avoided the police while staying close to Mass General in the hopes of getting in to see Crystal. The last time he had seen her was almost a week ago when the police found her in the underground building. She had been sick, and he learned it was poisoning, just like Ruth. He felt it was his job now to warn everyone.

Trevor's early life had been a series of unfortunate events. He was arrested at age fifteen after being suspended from school for dealing drugs. At first it was only selling candy during breaks, but when he saw how easy it was to distribute, he changed his product. Kids were eager to try everything he offered, weed and even pills. When he was caught selling on school grounds, he was sent to a juvenile facility that housed other kids, some even arrested for murder.

He was sentenced to three years, enough time to get his GED and learn about street hustling. People didn't understand that detention centers and prisons were education facilities to learn about dealing, stealing, and extorting. Trevor believed he had enough skills to make a good living. When he was finally let out on parole, he was ready for business.

It started out small, selling only recreational drugs to offset the cost of living and his own drug use. For a couple years, Trevor maintained a reasonable living. He was able to rent a nice apartment and buy a car. He had money to eat at restaurants and buy new clothes from department stores. But then he made a wrong move. He decided that drug trafficking was a better way to earn money. He was careful enough not to traffic illicit or scheduled drugs, like cocaine, heroin, or meth, because he knew that prescription drugs like Adderall, Oxy, and Vicodin, were pricier and easier to sell. By the time he was caught, he was addicted to all these drugs.

Because he had a prior criminal history, his punishment was harsh. He was sentenced to 3.75 years in prison. That's when he decided to change his ways. He accepted the rehabilitation that was offered and finally got off drugs thanks to his daily dose of Suboxone to curb the pain. While in prison, he took advantage of the several courses offered, especially classes in social work. His goal was to learn how to work with vulnerable people in an effort to help them choose to live better lives. Populations who suffered due to poverty, discrimination, or other social injustices were his top priority. When he was finally released, his lack of income and family support forced him to join the homeless population, somewhere he could put his skills to good use. That was four years ago.

He hadn't planned to end up in Boston, it had only been a stopover on his way to Rhode Island where a homeless counseling center was located. But once he saw the conditions of tents set up in vacant lots, sagging chain link fences, and people carrying backpacks or oversized plastic bags while looking for shelter beds, he stayed. Trevor saw ranting, raving, and eating from garbage cans. Boston streets were home to staggering men and women, lone figures in apparent stupors who wandered around, yelling at cars, shooting up in doorways or standing stock still, arms hanging loosely, knees bent, having taken drugs to induce sedation. Some of the street people drank a gallon of vodka a day, while others drank yellow Listerine to get sedated.

Trevor set up his tent in a busy encampment and started to watch and listen. He heard heartbreaking stories, and eventually became a trusted friend to many, someone who paid attention to their needs. He was like a detective sometimes, warning them about illicit activity or where security cameras were located. He intervened in brawls and helped people get treatment to calm them.

And now he wanted to find the person who was killing his friends.

Alan and Enrique spent the morning going through murder book files to find similar crimes that involved beating and strangulation. Because the homeless population seldom reported crimes of this nature, they had to dig deep to notice any similarity. It was a good lead, but Alan wanted to be more focused on the several interviews and observations his officers had reported. He was thankful when his phone rang.

"Detective," began Dr. Meyers, "we're getting very concerned with these poisonings. Have you alerted the public?"

"We're doing a press conference in two hours. My Lieutenant has notified the press and he will cautiously advise everyone on the importance of not accepting food or drink from unknown sources. We'll be careful not to cause a panic."

Dr. Meyers had more concerns. "Detective, as you know, we still have two victims here at the hospital. I'm now worried that we might have a problem with security. I'm afraid Jane Doe might have been the victim of additional poison of some sort that caused her to go into cardiac arrest. We're testing this now. I don't know how this could have happened because we only allow our staff into her room."

Alan thought for a minute. "Do you suspect one of your staff to have done this?"

Dr. Meyers answered with an upset tone. "I certainly hope not... but we use temporary nurses on call to help at times. I'll send over the names of who was on staff that night."

"I appreciate that. One more thing, have you concluded that all the poisonings were arsenic?"

"Yes. Has your forensic team found any food or drink source at the locations where the victims were found?"

"Not yet. But the teenager who was poisoned said he got a bread roll from a homeless guy on the street that made him sick."

"I've got to go, Detective, I'm being paged." The doctor rang off.

Alan sat back in his chair to consider again the idea that a homeless person might be behind the murders. His suspicion had been that it was someone who wanted to eliminate the homeless problem. A do-gooder. He sent a message to Officer Lane asking if they had located Trevor Reynolds. The text came back quickly, "Not yet."

Carla and Sidney were meeting Alan for dinner. They had a favorite Mexican restaurant near Copley Plaza and the reservation was for 6:00. They were waiting at a table in the corner window when Alan showed up. After ordering their food and a bottle of red wine, Sidney asked Alan how the investigation was going.

"Did I tell you we have an FBI profiler helping us?" Alan raised his eyebrows and expected his friends to be impressed. Instead, they looked worried.

Carla spoke first, "Why? Is this a federal crime? Is it because a police officer was murdered?"

"Yes, and yes. Agent Lee will be working with us in full capacity. He's already given us some good leads."

Carla looked interested. "What's he like? I think about all the profilers in books and on TV series and they all seem odd."

Alan gave a short laugh. "You would like him. He's Korean and very young. He dresses like he just stepped out of an ad for GQ which makes me look like a bum. But he's very intelligent and precise. I hope his profiling brings us closer to finding the suspect."

Sidney wanted to report about the abandoned building. "The city boarded up the building you told me about. I went over to make sure it had happened and found several people standing around. They said they had things inside the building and so I called someone to help them, but I didn't hear back. Hopefully, they retrieved their things before the building was closed off. You know, even in a decrepit place like that, it's still a roof over your head."

Carla then added, "I met with the teen boys at the

hotel. You were right, they should have been placed in foster care, but the social worker couldn't find homes. They have bus passes and I told them how to get to my center and so far, only one has shown up. I'm going to send one of my staff over to the hotel tomorrow to follow up. How's the teen in the hospital?"

Alan related what he knew. "I guess he'll be released over the weekend. Did you see the press conference an hour ago?"

Sidney nodded. "If there's someone who's targeting the homeless population, do you think it will stir up anger in their groups?"

"We're concerned about this. We have patrols around the encampments looking for any strange behavior. But now that the idea is out in the open, there may be copycat offenders around."

Their food arrived and the three friends changed the conversation to lighter subjects. Maggie's name came up several times, and Alan wished she lived closer. The Pacific Northwest seemed far away.

Ethan West was going crazy. The news report had everyone on edge and now he would have to back off his plan and lie low. It had been so easy to poison those lazy, worthless people, but he knew he had to be cautious, or he might get caught. Although he never left any clues, someone might suspect him just because he hung around the dirty shelter. He had to consider his options. Maybe it was time to throw the suspicion onto someone else. But who?

FRIDAY, FEBRUARY 7TH

An overnight winter storm had left drifts of snow piled up in the city. There were darkening skies, frozen streets, and a slick coat of ice gleaming over brick and stone. Connie and Sasha met for coffee near the precinct to review their agenda for the day. "We've looked everywhere for Trevor Reynolds, and he seems to have disappeared," Connie commiserated. "Maybe we should go back to the shelter and talk with Levi again." She looked outside and saw tiny snowflakes beginning to fall. "It's not going to be an easy day because of the weather. On the other hand, maybe we'll be able to talk with more street people who are seeking shelter."

Sasha seemed distracted. She tapped her fingers on the table and eyebrows drawn together. "Trevor is only a person of interest. We know he exists on the margins of society, but from what we've learned, he's a friend to almost everyone we talk to. I looked up his profile again and even though he was arrested for drugs, he's in treatment of some sort because he's on a prescription for Suboxone. I think people are helping him hide from us."

Connie nodded. "So maybe we should change our approach. Let it out that we need his help. I have an idea... let's start looking at the bus terminal by the shelter. It's so cold and with any luck we might find him there, in the crowd."

When the officers arrived at the bus terminal station, they noticed a young girl approach three men cautiously. The men were older, probably closer to her grandfather's age, and they were looking at the girl with concern. Because it was cold inside the terminal building, the men wore heavy jackets, the oldest of the group even had a down vest under his long heavy wool coat. It was difficult to see their faces clearly because they all wore hats, one had ear flaps on a plaid hat, another wore a baseball cap and the third man had on a knit hat that seemed tight on his head.

The girl they were talking to could be a schoolgirl with her dark green oversized sweatshirt and a backpack slung onto her shoulders. Her scuffed sneakers were soaked, and her jeans were wet at the cuffs. She had her hood up, but her braids had come loose from lack of attention.

"Do you need some help?" The man in the knit cap asked. He had a backpack on too, that looked heavy.

"I need a place to stay," she said quietly. "I missed my bus home." She was lying, but she had no choice. Any information she gave them had to be a lie so they wouldn't suspect she was running away.

"There's a hostel a couple blocks away," the older man said, "But I'm not sure it's still open or if it has a vacancy." He was studying her, and she wondered if he was a social worker or some kind of counselor. His voice was deep and filled with understanding. "How old are you?" he asked.

"Eighteen," she lied.

The man in the baseball cap shook his head slowly. "It's freezing out today and every place is probably full... even shelters. But I'll tell you something. This station keeps open if it dips below freezing, and it becomes a sort of shelter, even for the night. You can probably stay here."

The girl nodded and began to walk away just as the women officers approached the group. The men stood back and looked worried. One of them spoke up, "I think this young lady needs some assistance."

Sasha nodded and asked the frightened girl, "What do you need?"

The girl started to back away, but Connie stepped beside her and put a hand on her arm. "It's okay... we just want to know if we can help with something."

"I was just asking these men if they knew of a place I could stay because I missed my bus." The girl looked tearful. When Connie asked to see her ID, she brought out a student ID card from a high school miles away.

"Where are you going?"

"I've got an aunt who lives in North Hampton, and I'm going to stay with her."

Connie and Sasha looked at each other... probably another runaway. They motioned for the men to go on with their day and asked the girl to accompany them to the precinct. This wasn't how they planned their day to go. And they hadn't seen Trevor Reynolds at the station.

Trevor stood outside the shelter and watched Ethan talk with a few of the guys in line. There was something about the guy that Trevor didn't trust. He had met guys like him in prison, those who thought they were better and smarter than everyone else. They always made Trevor feel stupid just to prove they were superior by challenging him to some sort of game he couldn't win. He had warned his friends about people like that who manipulated conversations so they could cause a lot of confusion. Since you're homeless, you need support, not game playing or judgment. Trevor was going to keep focused on this volunteer.

Because the weather was dipping into the low twenties, Ethan knew the clinic would probably be closed. Those who needed medical care would have to go to Urgent Care at Mass General to receive treatment. His decision to drop by the shelter and see if anyone was discussing the news report about the potential poisoning was just a precaution. Word usually traveled quickly throughout the camps, and he wanted to hear what they suspected. He also needed a scapegoat or some way to devise a plan to insure his anonymity. He kept worrying about sneaking into Mass General that night to give an extra dose to that woman. He thought he had escaped the CCTV cameras but wasn't certain. He decided to go home.

Trevor hoped not to be noticed when he decided to follow Ethan as he left the shelter. All he wanted to know was where Ethan lived.

The streets were dangerous because of the ice and light covering of snow, but Ethan walked at a fast pace, showing more authority than he felt. Almost running down the subway tunnel, he saw his train arrive on time. Behind him, Trevor kept up and entered the next car, keeping his eye on Ethan. Because of the weather, the Greenline D was not crowded, which made it easy to see when Ethan got off at the T stop. Trevor followed him to a neighborhood close to Brookline Village.

Ethan had rented a studio in an overpriced building because of the space, which included a large living area with an alcove for a table and chairs. But it was the storage room off the balcony that pleased him. He had a place to keep his chemicals out of sight.

Trevor saw Ethan enter the building and wasn't sure why he needed to know this location, but his intuition told him it was important. Shaking his head, he turned to walk back to the train. He failed to notice a curtain open on the second floor and someone staring at him.

Agent Lee had spoken with several officers at the precinct and wasn't surprised to find that most officers didn't know any details about Officer Wagner. Being loyal to their team, they spoke with respect and regret that someone so young had been killed. Lee then spent time with Lloyd Randell in pathology to review the case. Evidence under Wagner's fingernails proved inconclusive because the suspect probably wore heavy clothes and gloves. But they did get a cloth sample from a coat. It looked like a heavy piece of wool, navy, and probably from a pea coat like most Bostonians wore in severe weather.

"Have you received the lab work from the poisonings yet?" Lee asked.

Lloyd scratched his head and said, "Well, that's the thing, this process takes time. And a positive result of arsenic doesn't necessarily mean the person was deliberately poisoned. Everyone can have a trace of arsenic in their systems. But because the symptoms were similar in the cases, we had to look for similar angles. It takes time to interpret these findings and run more tests."

"Are you at least conclusive in your report that arsenic was found in all cases?" Lee wanted to be certain.

"Yes. And from what I understand, it was given to the victims in a high enough dose to affect the digestive system."

Lee thanked Randell and went looking for the Detectives.

Alan was voicing his frustration with the encroaching weather and the slow pace of the investigations, when Agent Lee knocked on his office door. He was glad to see both detectives there.

"I hope you have some positive leads, Lee, because we seem to be getting nowhere." Alan motioned the agent to the chair beside his desk.

"I'm still reviewing the evidence. I've begun searching similar cases and I'm continuing to focus on your homeless poisonings. Can you tell me what you found about the other crimes in the nearby community where Officer Wagner was killed and what cases he was involved in."

Alan took out a folder on his desk. "In the past month, there were six cases of smash and grab in the vicinity. The robbers used hammers to smash windows and then stole whatever they could get in minutes. Other than that, there were cases of shoplifting, and both these offenses were of low priority for the police. We just don't have the manpower right now."

Lee was writing this down. "What about the last few cases the Officer was working on?"

Alan let out a deep breath. "As I mentioned, the day before he was with Detective Mendez visiting the homeless shelters and encampments. I wanted Wagner to get involved because of his conservative attitude. And then he drove patrol with Officer Lane the day he was killed. I know you've spoken with her. Do you have any ideas where to look now?"

Lee seemed unconcerned with the Detective's obvious frustration. "Many crimes don't follow common motives or patterns, making the perpetrators less predictable and more difficult to apprehend. And sometimes motive is not specific to the victim, but rather focused on the crime." Lee took out his folder and referred to his notes. "I mentioned that it all appears impulsive, and the Officer responded with force. His personality suggests he's competitive and insists on being right. I'm working on the idea that it was someone the Officer knew or suspected was stealing or in some way caught his attention."

"Where do we go with your theory?"

"I spoke with Officer Erickson about the argument he had with Officer Wagner on the street that day. It was about his views on the homeless population, and so with that in mind, I'm thinking that Officer Wagner already felt angry when he might have been chasing after someone. His movements were quick and impatient. That leads me back to the poisonings you are experiencing in this community."

"But we didn't hear about the poisonings until Officer Wagner was killed."

"True. But you had a squad meeting about moving forward with a plan to become more proactive. You had Carla Tompkins in to speak to your group, and that means it was an open challenge. Let's say, you struck a chord with this officer. He felt a conflict because of his views of right and wrong, but also wanted to be a part of the team. This makes me believe he might have seen something or, in this case, someone in the homeless community, who he wanted to question."

Enrique interrupted. "If that's the case, this person may be gone with the wind by now. Why wait around and be caught?"

"So true, Detective. And for all of us who understand the flight pattern, it's exactly what we would do. But now let's consider someone who has nowhere to go. Someone who may be on drugs and trying to survive the life they have, not the one they wished for. The inhuman effort it takes to appear normal and a part of things that appear easy to others. The loneliness." Lee stopped for a moment as if considering that reality.

Alan also took some time before he asked, "What do you suggest?"

"I want you to consider having a member of your force join the homeless community and listen for clues and evidence to solve both cases."

Alan was impressed. Why hadn't he thought to do this? He had informers on the street, and he could approach them, and Carla certainly had teens who heard a lot of rumors. This was an entirely new angle to go with. "Thank you, Lee. Will you be able to help us with some interviews?"

"Yes, of course."

Enrique and Alan met later that day with the Lieutenant. Alan explained his plan to send someone out to infiltrate the camps and listen for clues to help with their investigations. He needed to have the superior officer's advice on the legality of this maneuver because the law sometimes limits the actions of the police department's means of catching a criminal.

"I don't see a problem, Alan, because this happens all the time. What I would advise is to send a seasoned officer who knows the codes better than the new recruits. And, I would suggest, a woman."

Enrique looked surprised. "Why would you say that?"

Alan quickly responded. "This person needs to be able to empathize with the people they deal with and the fact that female officers are less likely to use aggressive tactics, saves them from legal problems. In other words, remaining cool, calm, and communicative usually stops violence before it erupts."

The Lieutenant nodded. "It's true. I wish we had more women officers. They're flexible and have a less aggressive approach which ensures the safety of others."

Enrique agreed. "I hope we get more women on the force. Do you have anyone in mind, Alan?"

"Yes, I do. I worked with a woman who just retired in upstate New York. We went to the academy together and I heard she's become a private detective. I'll give her a call."

Sylvia Adams rented a small office in the downtown area in the city of Albany, three blocks from the Hudson River. She retired from the police force two years earlier, and convinced herself it was because of the increased crime rate in the city due to gun violence. But if she was honest with herself, she was tired of spending the years climbing the narrow ladder of police promotions to finally claim a spot as lead detective, not to mention years of chasing suspects and putting her life on the line. Now she was happy to spend her time in the private sector, dealing with process serving and workers compensation. Occasionally, she got divorce cases, but she preferred not to.

Sylvia had three grandchildren she adored. It seemed to be one of life's fringe benefits that you had more free time to spend with your grandkids, than you ever had with your children. Her two daughters had full time jobs and Sylvia's part-time work as a PI gave her the opportunity to help their busy families. She once read that grandparents who occasionally helped with childcare lived something like 37% longer. Sylvia smiled at the thought.

Lately, her workload was light. She was wrapping up a report for a union worker and seriously considering taking some time off. The weather was miserable, causing a cold snap that lasted for weeks bringing a mixture of snow and freezing rain. Sylvia wondered if it was time to take a cruise south for some sun. She had never been to Florida... but she hated Florida. She was laughing to herself when the phone rang.

"Sylvia? This is Alan Sharp from Boston."

"Alan! How are you... it's been ages!"

"I'm doing fine, busy as usual. How's your PI agency going?" Alan always got right to the point.

"Well, my friend, it's just me running the place. But I'm satisfied with it because I can work or not. How about the crime in Boston... keeping you on your toes?"

"It is. In fact, that's why I'm calling. I need a PI to go undercover for me and I thought of you. It's a job for someone who's seasoned and who knows the ropes. Are you interested?"

Sylvia hesitated. "That's not much to go on, Alan. What exactly are you talking about?"

Alan explained the poisoning that was plaguing the homeless population. And then he told her about Agent Lee and his suspicion that the murder of Officer Wagner had something to do with street people. "We're getting nowhere on this investigation. People are refusing to talk with us, which is understandable due to the police reputation here, or anywhere these days. I need someone to go undercover and listen to the street talk... not do anything heroic, just report back on what might help our investigations."

Sylvia took a minute to consider this proposal. "So, you want me to infiltrate the community to gain information. Do you have enough resources for this project?"

Alan knew this would come up. "What do you charge for your services?"

"My services range from $75 to $90 per hour. But in this case, I guess a retainer would work best. That is, if I decide to take this project on. You need to tell me more."

Sylvia listened to the requirements and problems associated with the investigation. She would only have to lie low and draw as little attention as possible. And not to cause suspicion, she would dress ragged and have a story of past years on the street. No one would know she was a PI, not even the Boston squad.

"When do you need me to start?"

Alan quickly replied. "Now. Are you free?"

Sylvia let out a loud laugh. "Alan... you are a devious one! Am I the first or the last one you called?"

Alan smiled into the phone and hoped she knew this. "You were the first and only. We're at a roadblock right now and I was hoping your schedule was open."

When they rang off, Alan went to see the Lieutenant to get the proposed retainer ready to send. Hopefully, they would only need Sylvia for a week or two.

SATURDAY, FEBRUARY 8TH

Alan woke early and made a large pot of coffee. He liked his coffee strong and he would need caffeine today. The temperature outside had dipped again, and he worried about the people who had to find shelter. He always had a comfortable place to live, even after his two divorces, and couldn't imagine the stress and despair someone must feel when that was taken away.

Today he had to call the Wagner's again and confess that they had no leads. Alan reviewed some things on his mind. Gary Wagner seemed to have been trying to change things in his life. His counselor was optimistic, and his friend Zoe also felt he was moving in a positive direction. Maybe Agent Lee was right, and Wagner had been pursuing someone who broke one of his several rules of conduct. Or... maybe he saw someone run down the subway tunnel and just went to investigate. The cord... someone had a cord with them. Who carries something like that? What did they need it for? The ME said it was an ordinary cord, and it made sense that people who lived on the street would have this with them, as opposed to a regular citizen. Alan remembered seeing a homeless guy near the crime scene days later, and he had a cord around his long hair. And Lloyd also said there was a piece of cloth found from a jacket, probably a pea coat. These

195

were the only clues they had. Unfortunately, forensics reported that the bullet found on the wall of the subway had been lodged there months ago. Not a lead.

Alan looked at his watch and knew it was too early to call Enrique. His partner deserved some family time, and he could wait until Monday to talk with him. Just then his phone rang.

"It's me, Sylvia. Do you have a minute?"

Alan was pleased to hear her voice. "Yes. What have you decided?"

"Of course, I'll help. I can be in Boston tomorrow. Where can we meet?"

Alan decided to meet her at a hotel in Peabody, far enough away for her to be anonymous. He would be there at 10:00am.

Alan called his Lieutenant and reported that Sylvia was on board. He would be meeting her tomorrow and she could be on the streets Monday.

Ethan didn't volunteer on Saturday. Too many others needed to fulfill their obligation of public service and used weekends due to ongoing busy schedules. Now he had time to plan his next move and look to set someone up as a scapegoat. Planting the poison around the camps should be easy enough, and he would think of a way to leave an anonymous tip with the police to lead them to the poison. He also had to deal with the guy who followed him to his apartment. Ethan knew the guy hung around the shelter, so he would keep an eye on him.

Ethan had a nagging feeling that things were getting out of his control. Maybe he should be smart and just leave town before someone suspected him. He had money stashed in a hidden account and could go anywhere.

He was surprised when his phone rang. "Hi, Ethan, It's Nick Grainger, and I'm wondering if you're free today. Since the weather is so miserable, the shelter is overflowing with people who need food and a place to stay. Do you have time to come in?"

Ethan was reluctant, but he agreed. "I can manage a few hours this afternoon if that will help."

Nick sounded relieved. "Thanks. Be careful getting there, the streets are bad today."

Trevor was alarmed when he saw Ethan arrive at the shelter. Now that he suspected him of something, he noticed the peculiar way he interacted with the shelter people. He seemed oddly detached, more like an observer than a helper. There was a superficial way about him... smiling without making eye contact and only pretending to listen to conversations. He seemed to have a disregard for everyone around him.

Trevor hid in the corner so as not to be discovered and watched Ethan's interactions. He thought he should leave, but he had a choice of staying warm or fighting the frigid weather. Just then, someone called his name.

"Trevor Reynolds?"

Trevor looked around and saw Detective Mendez walking toward him. "Can I speak with you?"

It was an innocent enough question, but Trevor turned away and looked for an escape. Unable to find one, he stared irritably at the Detective. He didn't want to have a conversation, and especially didn't need the attention. "What's this about?" he demanded.

Enrique sat down next to Trevor and tried to appeal to his better senses. "We've been looking for you, Trevor. Don't worry, you're not a suspect, but simply a person of interest who might have relevant information for our investigation. You're well known within this community and may be our only reliable source right now." Enrique let this sink in and then asked, "By the way, how's your friend Crystal?"

Trevor looked suspicious. "Why are you asking me?"

Enrique remained calm. "You were spotted outside Mass General, waiting to see her. You know she was poisoned, just like Ruth. There have been other poisonings, too. Do you have any idea who might be doing this?"

Trevor glanced at Ethan West across the room and hoped the Detective didn't notice. He felt a sense of danger, like being trapped and needing to escape. "I need to go." Trevor stood and walked quickly out the door, into the freezing weather.

Enrique sensed Trevor's trepidation and knew there was someone in the room who had upset him. Looking around, he saw several homeless people lounging at the tables, drinking hot coffee from paper cups. He also noticed the volunteers who were working behind the counter and wondered if one of them had worried Trevor. The two older women wouldn't be suspicious, but the other three workers might know something. Enrique walked over to ask a few questions.

Ethan saw the Detective approach the kitchen. He drew in a deep breath and turned to pour himself a glass of water, attempting not to convey the panic he was feeling. But then he heard his name being called.

"Mr. West... " Enrique recognized him as the one who

had questioned him at the volunteer meeting. "Can I ask you if you know the person I was just talking to?"

Ethan looked blankly over the Detective's head. "I'm not sure. What guy?"

Enrique believed this guy was giving off a weird vibe, not looking him in the eye. "His name is Trevor Reynolds. Do you know him?"

Ethan gave out a strange laugh and said loud enough for others to hear, "I don't know many of these folks, Detective. I'm just the help around here." When no one else smiled at this, he seemed to freeze up. "No, I didn't recognize him."

Enrique's intuition told him that this guy was hiding something. He wanted to question him further, but sensed he would get nowhere. So, he thanked the kitchen crew and left to go look for Trevor.

Alan thought about the Wagners. The phone call with them earlier had been difficult, and he heard the appalling weight of the murder they were carrying inside. Alan also heard anger in their voices, and he understood their frustration. It must be difficult not to be overwhelmed with feelings of hate and even revenge. Was it revenge they wanted or justice? Revenge was an emotional reaction with a profound desire to hurt someone. Justice, on the other hand, was about righting a wrong, bringing the person to accountability. And, in some way, justice was about closure. They were probably wondering why the police hadn't solved the case quicker, since their son was one of their officers.

Making himself another pot of coffee, Alan looked inside his refrigerator for something to eat. Six eggs, a half quart of milk, cheese, and an outdated yogurt were all that was left from his shopping trip last weekend. What would Maggie do? Make an omelet he guessed. Then he remembered that Sam had left a quick recipe for something he called a Dutch Baby, kind of a pancake. It seemed an odd name for food, but Alan rifled through his junk drawer to find the instructions. Pulling out several items of dubious use, he finally found the recipe. Luckily, he had all the ingredients and so he rolled up his sleeves and started to make his meal.

When the Dutch Baby was pulled out of the oven Alan was stunned by how much it had risen. It was twice the size he had anticipated and so he took a photo of it and sent it to Maggie with the text, "I'm officially a Dutch Baby champion!"

Alan was amused how little it took to learn something new.

SUNDAY, FEBRUARY 9TH

T revor was worried and decided to get away from the city. He made a two-mile icy trek to an encampment outside of the city where he had friends and would be safe. He heard that no one in this camp had symptoms of poisoning so he began suspecting that the person who was involved in this was targeting city dwellers. Once again, his thoughts focused on Ethan West. Maybe it was because of his lack of boundaries or how he attempted to manipulate by using some kind of charm that Trevor didn't trust him. He thought again about the guys like that in prison. He would have to do some digging to find out more on West.

Alan arrived at the hotel to meet Sylvia at 9:30 and was able to get early access to a room. The hotel was in the city of Peabody off Route 1, thirty minutes from Boston. It was cheap and conveniently located near four transit sites along with 24-hour front desk availability. He messaged Sylvia the room number and then waited. At exactly 10:00 there was a knock on the door. Alan was shocked to see a hunched over older lady leaning heavily on a wooden cane. She was wearing a ragged coat and carrying an enormous plastic garbage bag over her shoulder. "Hi Alan… it's only me." Sylvia smiled and Alan noticed she was missing her front tooth.

THE DEAD OF WINTER

Amused and pleased, Alan opened the door and let his friend into the room. She quickly took off her false tooth and coat and sat on the edge of the bed. "Do you think I'll pass?" They both laughed.

Over the next few hours, they went over the plan. Sylvia was to take the subway into the city around dinner time and find the shelter. She would ask for a room, but because of the cold weather, she would be told that the train station was the only place open for the night. That's where Alan wanted her to begin listening for conversations about the poisoning or the murder. At any time, she could return to this hotel room and rest. This would also be the place where she would call Alan and report what she heard. When he left her, Alan felt optimistic that she would be able to find something to move the investigation forward.

Enrique arrived at the precinct in the early afternoon. He wanted to follow up on his suspicions about Ethan West and find out what his connection to the volunteer group might be. Looking up his profile, he saw the obvious, where he grew up, went to school and his employers. He seemed to have worked for five different agencies as a traveling nurse and this brought up questions. Enrique decided to call a few places and find out what kind of an employee Ethan had been.

By the time Alan got to the precinct, Enrique had collected some interesting information. "Ethan West's track record is filled with negative input: he was in trouble at fourteen, got kicked out of school for fighting and poor impulse control, even went to Juvie, got therapy, on probation, went to boarding school, caught cheating and yet... sees himself as a victim." Enrique let this sink into Alan's thoughts, and then continued. "And this is enlightening... I spoke candidly with two floor managers at his former clinic work sites who revealed that West had been accused of theft and quit to avoid prosecution. The clinics didn't press charges because they didn't want the problem to go public. So, they just let it go."

"What kind of theft? Money?" Alan was curious now.

"No, apparently it was drugs. Strange things... get this... it could be a combination used to make poison."

This got Alan's attention. "Let's get him in here. Do you have the clinic address where he works?"

"I already called, they're closed today, but I have his home address."

The drive to Ethan's apartment took longer than expected due to the snow drifts on the roads. Some of the local streets were blocked off, and kids were using the snowy surface for sledding and throwing snowballs. Alan had not called ahead, hoping that Ethan would be there and cooperate. Besides, right now, all they had to go on was hearsay.

The apartment building was old and needed work, but so did several of Boston's inner-city structures. Traveling nurses like Ethan were getting good pay but still couldn't afford to live in the city. That was another issue to bring to the attention of voters who complained about health care. When they rang the buzzer for Ethan's apartment, there was no reply. Where would he be on a cold Sunday late afternoon? The skies were grey, and the threat of another storm seemed imminent.

"Let's go to the shelter and see what his schedule is for the coming week. Maybe we can catch him there." Alan knew it was a long shot. He sent a message to Sylvia with a photo of Ethan West, telling her to let him know if she saw him.

Alan and Enrique arrived at the shelter just as the doors were closing. Showing their badges, they were let in, and Deacon Martin led them to a table. "We had to close because no one showed up to help. Usually, we stay open a few extra hours, but this weather has our volunteers stuck at home. Can I help you with anything?"

Alan looked around at the empty room and asked, "Have you seen Ethan West today?"

"He was here yesterday. He doesn't usually work on the weekends, but Nick called around to our volunteers because we were so short staffed. Why do you need him?"

"We just have a few questions. Is he scheduled for this coming week?"

Levi stood and walked over to the kitchen wall where schedules were posted. "It looks like he'll be here tomorrow at 5:00 and Wednesday, same time. He usually does the evening shift because of his job."

The Detectives thanked the Deacon, and as they were walking out the door, Enrique stopped and asked, "What have you heard from your people about the poisonings?"

Levi shook his head and responded, "Not much. Problems stay in their community. People are here to eat, get warm, and hope for a bed. I asked a couple of regulars what they had heard, and they just shrugged."

Alan and Enrique walked quickly to their car. It was getting late, and the cold air was bone-chilling. Alan hoped Sylvia had found a warm place to settle.

Sylvia saw the message and photo from Alan just as she left the hotel. She pulled a scarf tighter around her neck as she walked to the nearby subway using her cane to steady herself on the icy street. People were already avoiding her because of her disheveled appearance, and this pleased her. When she arrived at State Street, she looked around for street people, but there was no one. She walked to the shelter and found the doors were closed. A sign said to go to the South station for the night.

Trevor didn't notice the old lady who stumbled into the station. He was busy watching out for any sign of Ethan West. Things were getting complicated. Suddenly, he felt a tap on his shoulder.

"Do you know if someone like me can stay here?" The old lady spoke almost in a whisper.

"Yeah. It's open tonight. Just grab a space somewhere."

"I've got to get out of this city... I don't belong here..." Trevor heard the woman mumble.

"Where are you from?"

"Up north. Do you know Albany?"

Trevor nodded. "Sure... what are you doing here?" He looked at her tattered coat, old boots, and fingerless gloves. At least she had a cane for balance, but he wondered if she would survive the winter.

Sylvia stared at him. "Why do you need to know? You a cop or something?"

Trevor laughed. "Definitely not a cop. But if you're new to this city you should know that lots of folks don't have a place to go at night. You'd be best to keep moving."

"Hah! Like I have a choice!" She reached into her coat

pocket and brought out a granola bar. "Here... I have a couple more. They give them out where I come from."

Trevor took the bar and thanked her. Then he thought for a minute. "I want to warn you about something. Some people have been poisoned in the camps. We heard it was from food being given out... like rolls or bread... maybe even put in coffee or soup. So, it's best if you don't accept any unwrapped food."

She looked at him and gave him a toothless grin. "Thanks for the warning. Any one of your friends get poisoned?"

Trevor looked at her closely. Why did she want to know this? Was this a trap? But when he hesitated, he saw her turn and walk away. Maybe she forgot she even asked him a question. Why would he suspect an old lady? He continued to scan the crowd looking for West.

MONDAY, FEBRUARY 10TH

Agent Lee was waiting for Alan when he arrived at the precinct. Following the Detective to his office, Lee noticed that several police officers were at their desks, probably warming up before venturing out into the penetrating cold. This cold snap had been recorded as the coldest winter in twenty years, and the city was at a standstill.

"Close the door," Alan said as he sat behind his cluttered desk. Lee relaxed a little once the door was closed. "Have a seat while we discuss the case... cases."

Lee took out his iPad and was ready to take notes. Alan had seen him do this before and wondered at the younger generation who used a tech device instead of a notebook. If he were honest, he did understand the convenience, but Alan was locked into his old-fashioned ways and liked to write things down. To him, the written word had a personality.

"We now have an undercover person on the streets who will be reporting back to me. I hope this idea works and we can get some leads. In the meantime, we have an interest in one volunteer at the shelter who has a shaky background. He also has access to the hospital labs because he's a nurse at a clinic in town. So far, we haven't been able to contact him, but we're told he'll be at the shelter today at five."

Lee looked up from his computer, "Why don't you go to

his workplace?"

"It's closed due to the weather. Detective Mendez and I went to his apartment yesterday, but he wasn't there. I'm just hoping he hasn't decided to skip town."

"Can you give me some details about this person? Maybe it will fit into my profile of the murderer."

Alan related what he had learned about Ethan West and watched as Lee's fingers flew across his keyboard. Even on the best of days, Alan felt incapable of typing at a regular speed without searching for every key. Not to mention his resistance to the hundreds of other programs and skills the tech world could offer him.

"When you locate Ethan West, do you mind if I sit in on the interview? I wouldn't interfere, but I want to hear his answers." Alan agreed.

Lee stopped typing and then changed the discussion to Wagner's family. "From what you've told me, they're very conservative. This leads me to think Officer Wagner had unrealistic expectations and was filled with disappointment. You said he was critical of others and fixated on small details, and when others didn't fall in line with his plans, he became irritated. It sounds like he had difficulty accepting other possible outcomes."

Alan folded his arms across his chest. "Where does this lead us?"

Lee looked thoughtful. "I believe you're already on the right path with the homeless. This community does not follow the normal set rules the city dictates. This is an area that would probably frustrate Officer Wagner. Did you find out if he was following any investigation that dealt with the homeless?"

"Unfortunately, stores and businesses have been closed this week due to the weather. We know they've been frustrated with the homeless problems, people leaving garbage... and worse... outside their stores. If Wagner had a reason to talk about security or protection with any of the store owners, we haven't been able to contact them."

Lee continued to type and seemed to be working through other possible scenarios. "I'll get back with you in a few hours, Detective."

Just as Lee was walking out of his office, Alan's phone rang. It was Sylvia. "Alan, I'm back at the hotel. So far, I've spoken to Trevor Reynolds a couple of times, and I would be surprised if he were involved with the poisoning or the murder. He cares strongly for the people who suffer on the street and wants closure on the poisoning as much as we do. He told me about his friend Crystal. I guess she's still at Mass General. Probably a good place to be in this weather."

"Did you hear any talk about the murder?"

"Now, remember, I've only been listening for one night, but I did hear some bad mouthing about police interference. At first, I thought it was the usual criticism we always hear, but I noted a harshness and vindictive conversation by a few people. I have their names... Vince Robarts and Cal something... I didn't get his full name. Anyway, they seemed to be very angry."

"Vince Robarts was the one who found Officer Wagner on the platform. We need to bring him in again if he's out there causing trouble. That's a good lead. Are you going back soon?"

Alan heard a tired laugh. "I'm going to take a nap first. But I'll check in when I get back here later."

Vince Robarts. He wasn't a big guy, probably 5'6" and wouldn't have had the strength to kill someone as tall as Wagner. Robarts had a pointed beard two inches below his chin and balding fuzzy red hair, so he was easy to spot. At the time Alan spoke with him he thought his hooded eyes had seen a darker side of humanity which made him appear troubled. Robarts had found the body... they had interviewed him... did he keep something back? Was he trying to protect someone? Now Alan was suspicious and immediately called Officer Lane.

Over the weekend, Sasha had reviewed her notes on Wagner. She somehow felt responsible for not knowing more about him since they rode together the day he was killed. Was he quizzing her about police rules and personal style to get a rise out of her, or was he wanting to get her approval? If so, why? She had never had much interaction with him before, and in fact thought he was too conservative for the police force. But that wasn't her call to make. What else had they discussed?

When she received a message to report to Detective Sharp, she hoped it wasn't about Wagner. But she was wrong.

Alan offered her a chair and got to the point. "I want you to tell me again about when you first saw Vince Robarts. He ran into the restaurant... "

Sasha blinked and went back in her mind to sitting at the table with Connie. They were just finishing their wine when the door flew open. The homeless man had staggered in and yelled "Officer down" two times and then dropped to the floor. "We saw him hit the floor and went over to help. He was winded but kept pointing out the door. Someone gave him water and he sat up. I showed him my badge and asked him what he meant. He kept pointing and saying there was a dead officer in the tunnel. Connie and I each took an arm and asked the guy to take us to the tunnel."

"Did he resist?"

"Not really. He was breathing heavily and seemed weak. We walked him to the tunnel and down to the platform. That's when we saw the body."

"Where was Robarts at this point?"

"Officer Beale stayed with him as I approached the body and called for an ambulance and backup. We told Robarts to stay close while we began securing the crime scene."

"Did he stay?"

"At first, he tried to leave, but I advised him to remain and make a statement. By then other officers were on the scene and someone took him to the station."

"Did you think at any point that he knew Office Wagner or had committed this crime?"

Sasha raised her eyebrows. "I'm not sure. That's an interesting theory. I guess my only thought at the time was that he knew who did it and was afraid he might be blamed."

"We need to find him. Can you and Officer Beale make this a priority today?"

"Yes, sir. What about Trevor Reynolds? We haven't located him yet."

"I have someone else following him. Right now, concentrate on Robarts."

Vince Robarts glanced nervously around the small room that was filled with boxes. This was a good hiding place where no one usually looked. It was a storage space in an old building and Vince knew he could get a few hours' sleep before it was locked up for the day. His decision to stay hidden was due to his fear of one person. Vince knew who had killed the cop and heard that person was looking for him. If it wasn't for this icy grip of winter, Vince would be on his way south. He had friends who lived in warmer climates who could put him up for a while. That was how he spent his days... most of his life, really... wandering from place to place.

When Vince was a child, his father hit him repeatedly in the head, causing him to pass out and eventually lose concentration on normal activities. Failing at school and every other part of his life, he eventually ran away from home and somehow survived on the streets. A couple years ago he entered a treatment facility and was diagnosed with paranoid tendencies due to repeated head trauma. He was told it was probably the severe childhood beatings that caused his personality changes, impulsivity and poor decision making. That, and his love of alcohol, an addiction he could not escape.

Vince often spent days riding on 24-hour subway trains because of the adverse weather or just for shelter and comfort. It was on one of his long rides that he saw the cop get killed. When the lights had flickered in the dark tunnel before the stop, he saw the brutal murder and the guy ran away. Why was he the only one who noticed? Was everyone else too absorbed with the weather and their phones? Vince had jumped off at the stop and rushed to see if he could help. Now he had to stay hidden, from the police and the killer.

Sylvia didn't sleep well in the hotel because of the noise of the city. She was used to her small cottage by the lake in upstate New York where she woke up to the sound of birds. Now she lay awake and questioned why she decided to get involved with this investigation. One reason, of course, was because of her respect for Alan. She had watched his career over the years and admired his tenacity to solve cases along with the responsibility to build trust and confidence with the public. She also knew that if she needed his help, he would drop everything. She had to smile at the thought that they both had grandchildren now. Maybe it was time to slow down. Slowly, she drifted off for a few hours' sleep.

It was mid-day when Sylvia walked the few blocks to the subway. She wore an extra sweater to keep the chill from penetrating through her garments and huddled close to her oversized bag. She swayed back and forth on her cane as she waited for the subway because she knew it helped to keep moving. By the time she boarded the train, her fingers were numb, and her feet were cold. She almost sighed out loud as the heat of the car hit her head on. The twenty-minute ride was a deserved respite.

When Sylvia got off the train and started up Mass Ave, she saw a lone figure wearing a tattered pea coat and a cap pulled down over his forehead stumbling down the street towards her. He carried a heavy bundle of what might be his possessions and he stopped to bend over slightly and gasp for breath. He was obviously drunk or on some sort of drug induced high as he staggered and then fell into a light post.

A few people walked around the man without looking at him, probably hoping that someone else would come to his rescue. Sylvia knew that the homeless population in Boston had grown to such a number that they no longer expected help from anyone. Even asking for handouts on the street was no longer an option because people believed the media who told them that drug addicts just bought more drugs when given cash.

Sylvia watched from across the street as people passed by, ignoring the desperate man on the sidewalk. Taking out her phone, the burner that Alan said to use only in emergencies, she called him. "There's a guy in distress on Mass Ave, near Mousey Park. What should I do?"

Alan replied, "Stay where you are. I'll have officers there soon. Do you recognize the man?"

"Not from here. I'm worried he's having trouble breathing... I can see his breath from the cold air, and it looks like he's gasping."

"I've got EMTs on the way. Please stay where you are. I don't want you to get hurt if he's dangerous."

"I know... it's just difficult to stand here if he really needs assistance." Sylvia hung up and, huddling against the cold wind, waited until the ambulance arrived.

Vince Robarts knew he was in trouble when he began gasping for air. He noticed the woman across the street staring at him and hoped she would help but he couldn't call to her because of his tremors and inability to concentrate. The medics found him passed out on the street but were quick to revive him and check his alcohol level. It measured .11, which was well above the legal limit.

When Alan was alerted that Vince Robarts was in the hospital, he called Sasha and Enrique to meet him there. They had a lead at last.

Sylvia walked tentatively to the shelter once she saw the ambulance rounding the corner. The cold had reached inside her and even her breath felt icy. When she entered the shelter door, she imagined her disguise went unnoticed because she looked like all the other people there who needed a meal and a warm place to sit. Moving slowly to a vacant table, she rested her bag and cane on the floor and sat, giving out a loud sigh. A few people turned to look, but nobody seemed to care.

Sylvia noticed a young man who was speaking easily to some men sitting across the room from her. Although she couldn't hear the conversation, she watched as they acknowledged some shared comment with amusement. It surprised her to think that even on days as cold and threatening as this, they could still find some humor. To her, the extreme cold weather would have evoked despair. But, she considered, street people have amazing coping skills.

Deacon Martin noticed Sylvia sitting alone at the table and walked over to greet her. "Welcome, I believe you're new here." He put out his hand in friendship.

Sylvia took off her glove and shook his hand. "Yes, I'm just passing through. The weather has locked me in for a couple days."

Levi nodded. "I wish we had a bed for you here, but we're filled up. I'm sorry. But please stay for a meal."

Sylvia took this opportunity to ask him a few questions. "It's okay, I spent last night at the train station. When I was there, I was talking with a guy named Trevor and he said there's been some poisoning going on. What do you know about that?" Sylvia tried to appear worried rather than investigative.

Levi sat down and shook his head. "Folks here are starting to get worried. I guess a few of their friends have died! Right now, I just try to calm everyone down and reassure them that they're safe here."

"Any rumors? Trevor said something about people handing out food that's bad." Once again Sylvia looked apprehensive.

Levi nodded. "From what I've heard, it comes from someone on the street... who looks innocent enough but is up to no good. Worse... killing people."

Just then Levi noticed Ethan walking in the door. "I've got to go... " he said to Sylvia.

With a quick glance over her shoulder, Sylvia recognized the person Levi was talking to. It was Ethan West... the guy Alan was looking for to interview. She decided to wait and watch. Ethan was speaking quickly to Levi and, looking around the room, turned and then left. Sylvia picked up her things from the floor and followed him.

Ethan was worried. If the police wanted to talk with him, like Levi said, he needed to find a place to lie low and think this through. He couldn't safely get out of the city for fear of being noticed. Most transportation systems were at an emergency level which meant that CCTV cameras could easily find him. He was certain they knew where he lived by now, so he had to find another place. The clinic was nearby, and even though it was closed, he had a key. That's where he could hide.

Sylvia followed Ethan at a distance. He was walking at a slow pace, probably thinking over his next move if the Deacon told him the police wanted to talk with him. It was reasonable to believe that he might know something about the poisoning because of his involvement with the shelter. She watched as he turned on to State Street and quickly picked up his pace.

When he reached the corner, Sylvia tried to catch up, but as she peered down the next street, he was gone. She looked up at the stores and noticed a light go on in one shop. It was the downtown nurse's clinic. Pulling out her burner phone, she dialed Alan.

When Ethan heard the police sirens outside the building, he remained cool headed until the police arrived and demanded that he open the door. Like most psychopaths, Ethan West lived in fear of being caught. On the other hand, he was reckless and had little regard for private property or social norms. In fact, he enjoyed the thrill of getting away with something, breaking the rules and even liked the fact that he might get caught one day. He planned to rationalize his behavior and say his decision to break into the clinic had been impulsive due to the extreme weather.

He was lucky he had kept his relationship with his colleagues on a superficial level and would be able to manipulate and take advantage of their understanding. When he opened the clinic door, he pretended to act remorseful.

TUESDAY, FEBRUARY 11TH

Alan remained cautious, but hoped they were getting closer to an arrest. He and Enrique had arrived and charged Ethan West with illegal entry at the clinic and kept him locked up overnight. They were scheduled to interview him but met first to decide what information they needed. Alan was frustrated. "We don't have a reason to keep him if the clinic isn't going to press charges. When I talked with the supervisor, she told me he wasn't allowed in after hours, and he would be put on probation while they sorted out why he was there. When we picked him up, he said something about being too cold and looking for shelter. Otherwise, he wasn't talking."

Enrique shook his head. "This guy seems really sketchy. If it's true he has a history of stealing drugs, maybe we should get a warrant for his apartment. Could be he was using the clinic to get more supplies."

Alan agreed and made the call. "Now let's go and see what he has to say."

Ethan had spent the night in a cell with two other men. He knew not to speak to anyone and needed time to formulate some answers to the questions the police might ask him. It was stupid of him to go to the clinic. He hadn't been thinking clearly and was angry with himself.

When he was led into an interview room, both Detectives were present. After introducing themselves for the recorder, Ethan was asked to state his name. He realized this might be more serious than he expected. If he said too much, there might be a hasty indictment even though there was no evidence that he did anything wrong. He hoped there was no evidence.

Alan began the questioning. "Mr. West, what were you doing at the clinic last night?"

Ethan stared back, "I was seeking shelter."

Alan nodded. "Why didn't you just go to your apartment?"

"I thought I was getting sick."

"Too sick to make it home?"

"Yes."

Enrique looked sternly at Ethan. "What do you know about the poisoning that's happening in the homeless community?"

"Nothing."

"We have a warrant to search your apartment. Do you want to comment on this?"

Ethan sank further into the chair and asked for an attorney.

It was over.

Sylvia was back at the hotel after spending another night at the train station. She didn't see Trevor there but watched and listened to conversations. Her heart ached as she saw families with young children try to bed down for the night. If only the wealthy politicians would spend a night or two in this place and see the need. Maybe they would stop talking about doing something and pass some laws that helped.

Alan called her just as she lay down to rest. "Thank you for your help, Sylvia. Ethan West has been arrested for the poisoning. We found the poison he used in a storage room in his apartment. He was arrogant enough to hide it in plain sight, just like any psychopath would... thinking they were smarter than anyone else. He's been charged for murder."

Sylvia was pleased. "Do you still want me to circulate?"

"For a couple more days. We're going to interview Vince Robarts and see what he knows about Wagner's murder. My guess is that he's kept something from us... something he saw. Are you okay with continuing your watch?"

"Sure. Although I have to say, Alan, I'm feeling such heartache for the people who live like this. I guess I had no idea. I mean, we all see street people and feel sorry for a minute and might even stop and give out a few dollars... but then we just continue with our privileged lives. We vote in people who promise to take care of this, but who never follow through. I'm at fault, too, for this because sometimes I honestly feel numb to the suffering."

Alan listened and felt tired and dispirited. He knew there were problems in the healthcare systems, public health, housing, welfare, education, and legal and correctional systems. He and his team did their best to try to keep the city safe, patrolling and responding to emergencies, protecting citizens and property, investigating, and preventing crimes, enforcing laws... the list goes on. He knew Sylvia understood this. "You know I agree with you. And I'm sorry to have put you in such a position. Once again, when you go out, don't put yourself at risk. Call me if you need assistance." Alan knew Sylvia wouldn't let him down.

THE DEAD OF WINTER

When Trevor heard the news that Ethan West had been arrested, he breathed a sigh of relief and returned to the shelter for the evening meal. Levi met him at the door. "Glad to see you, Trevor. Any news on the street?"

Trevor gave a slight shake of his head and headed for a table. He liked the Deacon, but never wanted to spend time in conversation with anyone who worked there. He looked around for familiar faces and noticed the old lady he had talked with at the station. She asked a lot of questions, but he guessed he would too if he were new to a city.

Sylvia saw Trevor look her way and nodded. If he wanted to talk with her, she would let him approach, otherwise he might suspect something because of her questions. He seemed intelligent. Just then the door flew open, and someone yelled, "We have a cop watching us! Everyone needs to be careful!"

The room went silent. "What? How do you know?" Someone yelled back.

The man held his arms up in the air and waved them frantically. "We just know! They're following us and arresting us! They got Vince!"

Sylvia stopped breathing for a minute. Did someone see her talking with Vince at the station? She looked the other way and tried to shrink down into her chair. Everyone was focused on the man who was shouting and maybe she could stay unnoticed. She recognized who he was… it was Cal. He and Vince Robarts were friends.

Alan and Enrique arrived at the hospital in the evening to speak with Vince Robarts. They were told he was recovering from an overdose of drugs and alcohol but was awake. Robarts looked startled as if disoriented when he saw the officers enter the room. He tried to sink lower in the bed and clear his mind from the medication the doctor had given him to ease the drugs in his system.

"Mr. Robarts, we have some questions for you." Alan began, "Let's go over the evening you found Officer Wagner dead on the platform. Where were you coming from on the train?"

"I don't remember," he muttered.

"We need some answers, sir, because we believe you know more than you're telling us. We think you're hiding something that might help us find a killer. And if you help us, we'll help you." Alan kept his eyes glued to the man.

Robarts was afraid that the information he had kept from the police was running around in his brain and would eventually surface. He was frightened and didn't know who to trust. "I guess I was just on a ride. When the weather's bad like this, I stay on the train until I get kicked off."

"Okay... so you were riding and then saw the officer. Who else did you see?" Alan spoke firmly, knowing that Robarts was acting fidgety, and probably had something to hide.

"I might have seen someone. But I'm not sure... but I heard that a guy is after me!" Robarts looked nervously at the officers.

"Who is it?" Alan asked with authority. Now they were getting somewhere.

Robarts felt drained. He hadn't done anything wrong in the first place. It was time to give into the pressure. "He was a regular guy... you know, not like a street person. He seemed angry and I saw him smack the officer and then pull out a rope and strangle him!"

"Describe this guy," Enrique pulled out his notebook.

"He was almost as tall as the cop, wearing a navy coat... you know, like everyone wears... and had on a knit hat. That's all I saw."

"Why did you get off the train and go to help?" Enrique questioned.

Robarts shook his head repeatedly. "I don't know. I guess I was upset and kind of in shock. I wanted to help the guy on the ground."

"Did you see the other guy run off?"

"No, by the time the train stopped he was gone."

"Have you seen him since? Has he ever been to the shelter?"

Robarts shook his head frantically. "I don't know... but like I said, someone's looking for me."

Alan thought about this. Robarts was not tall, but his reddish hair and beard would make him a better target. "Who knows you're here now?"

"All my friends. They saw the ambulance pick me up."

Alan turned to Enrique, "Let's get a guard here."

Deacon Martin overheard Cal come running into the shelter and yelling. Now that he knew where to find Vince Robarts, he made a phone call to report.

Nick Grainger sat in his cramped office and considered his next move. He was worried.

WEDNESDAY, FEBRUARY 12TH

Agent Lee was waiting for Alan at his office door. He looked eager to talk, and Alan hoped he had some new ideas. Having Ethan West in custody was a relief, but Alan couldn't rest until he brought in the killer of his officer.

"Did you hear we got the guy who poisoned all those people?" Alan asked Lee.

"I just found out. He matches the profile I have, a psychopath who believes he'll never get caught. Having the drugs at his apartment is a sure sign of arrogance. He thought he was above the law."

Alan nodded. "Now we're back to finding the killer of Officer Wagner."

Lee handed Alan a folder. "I've broken down the case. You say you interviewed Vince Robarts, tell me what he said."

Alan remembered that Lee had asked to be present when he talked with Robarts. "I'm sorry we didn't bring you along... it was getting late. He's afraid someone's after him. Apparently, he saw more than he originally told us. The guy who killed Wagner was tall, had on a knit cap and a pea coat and moved quickly. He was gone by the time Robarts got there."

Lee thought for a moment. "My ideas continue to focus on the homeless. If Officer Wagner made someone so angry with his admonishment of street people, there is the possibility that he was targeted. It may be someone unconnected to the community, or someone who has strong beliefs about helping in some way."

Alan immediately stood up. "Wait a minute... are you saying that it might be a volunteer? Because Officer Wagner was planning to volunteer with the homeless shelter according to his therapist."

"That would be a good place to start. My guess is that he couldn't begin any volunteer program without training. Are the volunteers trained?"

"According to the director, it's solid training. But as far as I know, the only opportunity Wagner had to talk with someone was the day he was killed. He had taken the afternoon off and had an appointment somewhere. We never found out where that was."

Lee nodded and looked at Alan who was now pacing the floor. "Can I help in any way?"

"You've already given me quite a good lead. I want you to go and speak with Vince Robarts and see if you can find out any other details from his memory of that day."

Alan called Enrique.

"I ran ID on all the volunteers Grainger had on the list he gave me, and they all came up clean. I know the guy vetted them and so I didn't expect to find anything."

"And yet... Ethan West seemed to have made his way into the program. I wonder how he did that."

"Let's go talk with Grainger." Enrique looked at his watch. It was already past noon and maybe they could catch

Grainger before he decided to close because another storm was scheduled to hit the city.

Nick Grainger was used to conflict. He had been raised by parents who were loud and abrasive and had learned at a young age how to navigate around those types of personalities. Being their only child, he was often caught between his parents' arguments and managed to find comfort by spending hours playing video games. Because gaming demanded his focus and concentration, sometimes he forgot to eat or sleep, not that his parents noticed.

By the time Nick was in middle school he was addicted to the games. He lacked any motivation to engage in other activities and eventually his grades began to suffer. His school attendance also began to decline because he was often sick with tension headaches due to prolonged screen time. When he graduated from high school, he finally realized that gaming had become his entire identity, and he admitted he had a problem. He started to read up on how video games affected a person's body, brain, and nervous system. Even when he stopped gaming for a month as an experiment, the urge to play would become overwhelming, and he started up again. That's when he turned to self-help videos and podcasts to learn how others quit or at least limited their hours in front of the screen.

Nick understood he needed to get away from the games and stay busy. He enrolled in a local community college as a distraction to keep his mind off the games and began socializing in the real world. After a while, his gaming was down to a few hours on the weekends and sometimes he even missed those hours. He started to make friends and ended up volunteering for an outreach program sponsored by the school. That started him on the road to a degree in social work and psychology. He graduated from a four-year college by the time he was twenty-four, and continued his studies, eventually earning a master's in political science. By that time, he identified several avenues to pursue in his ambitious future.

It wasn't in Nick's plan to move to Boston five years ago. In fact, he hated the winter weather that lasted for months. But when the job was offered to run a volunteer organization for the city, he thought it would be a good start for his political future. Boston was filled with opportunities and Nick was young and eager to learn.

Ethan West heard of Nick from the other nurses at the clinic. They were impressed with Nick's dedication to the homeless and Ethan thought that might be a good way to get closer to that community and fulfill his plan. Joining the list of volunteers was easily accomplished when he mentioned to Nick that he was a part-time gamer. Once that door was open, Ethan and Nick began meeting online each week and playing video games. By this time, Nick had returned to gaming and even considered it a competitive sport. They lied to each other saying this was the only time they indulged in this guilty pleasure, but both men were busy gamers.

Nick was angry at himself. Now that Ethan had been arrested, the focus was going to come back on him. He had to be careful. Nick was nervous because he hadn't gone to the trouble of vetting Ethan like other applicants because they were friends and Nick felt it was unnecessary to go to all the trouble. After all, Ethan was a nurse, and the clinic had already looked over his records. Why was Ethan arrested?

When the Detectives arrived at his office, Nick saw the seriousness of their faces and felt himself break into a cold sweat. He tried to feign impatience as he led them out of his small office and to a larger room with a conference table and chairs.

Alan slowly took out his notebook and pencil, hoping to put more pressure on Nick. "We're here to ask you some questions about one of your volunteers. Did you vet Ethan West when he applied as a volunteer?"

Nick pursed his lips and shook his head. "I'm sorry to say I did not. Sometimes a person comes along and with their background I just pass them through. Ethan is a nurse and I considered that the clinic had vetted him."

"He has quite a record." Enrique said.

Trying not to appear defensive, Nick shook his head. "I'm sorry to hear that. He always seemed to be an upright kind of guy. It was my mistake to let that slip."

Alan continued his questioning. "Did Officer Wagner have a meeting with you to sign up as a volunteer?"

Nick was surprised when he heard the officer's name and quickly nodded. "I have his application."

"Did you speak with him?"

"Yes, but only for a short while."

"Do you remember what day?"

Nick's shoulders lowered. "No. But I remember it was the week he was unfortunately killed. He seemed anxious to start volunteering right away."

Enrique looked confused. "Do you let someone start without training?"

"Well, that's the thing. He seemed upset that he couldn't get started the next day. I told him about the training, and he walked out."

Alan frowned and looked uncertain. "You didn't see him again?"

Nick shook his head.

Enrique studied him and wondered why Grainger had such bloodshot eyes. Maybe he was working late hours, but he was also avoiding eye contact. Was he hiding something? Or lying? Something was off. "Do you have a copy of the application?"

"Yes, of course. Do you want to see it?"

Enrique nodded and watched Nick as he offered a flash of a smile that didn't reach his eyes. "I'll be right back."

Alan's eyes narrowed and he knew something was up. "Have we looked into this guy? I get the feeling he's being vague about West, and he seems overly anxious."

Nick entered the room with a file folder and handed it to Alan. "It's not much. The officer was going to return to complete the form."

Alan glanced at the written application and then back at Nick. "What is it that you're not telling us? How do you know Ethan West?"

Heaving a sigh, Nick decided he had to be truthful. "We're gamers. That's how I got to know him. Right now, we're competing in online games a few nights a week. So, when he said he wanted to be a volunteer, I didn't bother vetting him. Now I regret it."

"You mean video games... right?" Alan asked. Nick nodded.

"Okay, I'll need a list of the games. Is there anything else you want to tell us?" Alan was feeling even more convinced he was hiding something.

Nick shifted his weight and wondered how to proceed. In fact, he seemed to have lost the ability to process the situation or find the words needed. Finally, he said, "I don't know anything more to tell you."

The officers followed Nick back to his office for the video game information. Alan looked around the small office and saw a pea coat hanging on a hook. Everybody had one.

When the detectives left the office, Alan needed to talk. "I guess the whole gaming world is more insidious than I thought. Maybe you know more about it."

Enrique shook his head. "Only what I read or hear online. We let our girls play the shopping games, but maybe we need to stop that. My guess is they play games at their friends' houses anyway. One problem is that you don't know about another parent's restrictions on gaming."

Alan changed the subject. "Our evidence is still lacking. We only have speculation so far on the murder and that's not leading us to any solid clues. Let's go back to the office to see if the trail might come together with another look."

Sylvia left the shelter and returned to the hotel. She had to think this through. Now that Ethan West was in custody, she decided to concentrate on the murder. She called Alan.

"I'm wondering what you want me to do now that you have West."

"To bring you up to speed, we talked briefly with Vince Robarts, and we just left Nick Grainger's office. These men remain people of interest. Agent Lee is convinced that the homeless community is somehow involved with the murder, but I can't put my finger on why or how. Are you willing to keep trying to find more information?"

"Yes. But, you know, I doubt that people who are struggling with so many problems themselves, are necessarily out to hurt anyone. Maybe your culprit is just an ordinary citizen with cop-hating beliefs. Although, I suppose that would include half of the city." Sylvia let out a short laugh.

Alan shook his head, understanding what Sylvia meant. "I appreciate what you're doing to help us. Enrique and I are going over the files right now, and I'll let you know if we come up with anything." They agreed to check in later.

Both men were deep in thought about Officer Wagner's murder and had little to say. Too much time had elapsed, and they knew the longer this dragged on the less chance they had to find the killer. Usually, by this time in an investigation, they had the suspects dwindled down to three or four.

Looking at the incident board, they only had Wagner's associates, family, and some background. "What about the academy? Did anyone come through on who might have had a beef with Wagner?" Enrique asked.

"I had an officer call around and it turned up nothing. We already knew he had some personality problems, but we also know he was trying to get help."

"He lived by himself, had a new friend, Zoe, but was still looking at profiles online. Did anything show up on his computer?"

"Not much. But remember his sister said he had another phone." Alan thought for a minute and then made a call to the tech department. "Did you ever find another phone listed for Officer Wagner?"

"Let me look," came the young voice on the other end. "Yeah, we found another number. Do you want me to send that to you?"

"Yes, thanks." Alan shook his head. "I should have followed up on this."

When his computer lit up, Alan turned it towards Enrique so they both could try to find a clue. There were several calls to his sister, and a few to a number unrecognized. Alan called this number.

"Hello, how can I help you?"

"I'm calling for Gary Wagner, who am I speaking with?"

"You have reached the City Councils line; how can I direct your call?"

"Is it possible to reach Nick Grainger on this line?"

"Yes, would you like me to connect you?"

"No, thank you." Alan hung up.

"Why do things keep pointing back to this guy?"

Enrique agreed. "Let's run a check on him."

Sylvia bundled up before leaving the hotel. She had on three pairs of socks and two pairs of gloves. Inside her pockets were hand warmers which she relied on. Tonight, she would stay at the station and try to roam around and listen. She had to overcome her desire to comfort the people she saw, those whose faces were fixed as if all the joy had been squeezed out. They were only surviving the life they had, not the one they wished for.

Right away she noticed Cal and Trevor talking to each other. She would have to steer clear of them in case they thought she was the one who had named Vince Robarts to the police. Just then someone tapped her shoulder. "I think you're the one he's looking for?" The man was pointing to Trevor. "You better watch out... Cause he's plenty mad!"

Sylvia turned away and started toward the door. Just

then she heard a loud voice, "Hey! You! I want to talk with you!"

Frozen by the loud outburst, Sylvia reached in her pocket for her phone. But a hand reached out and tried to grab it. "Who are you calling? The police?" Trevor was by her side looking angry.

"No, my phone doesn't even work. I just use it for security." Sylvia had turned her phone off in the attempt to make it useless. She held it up for him to see the blank screen.

"Who are you really?" Trevor was causing a scene and several people were approaching them.

"I already told you... I'm trying to get out of the city and back to Albany. I'm stuck here because of the storm... just like everyone else!" Sylvia tried to appear exhausted to garner some pity from the big man.

Trevor was persistent. "Where do you go during the day? I only see you here at night."

"You saw me at the shelter. Why do you care?" Sylvia stared at him, attempting to accuse him of prying.

Trevor looked annoyed. In a sharp tone he stated, "We've got some serious problems with the police right now. Someone's been poisoning our friends and some of them think we killed that cop. There's a snitch hanging around here... we're going to find out who it is."

Sylvia just nodded. "Good luck." And she walked slowly away, leaning heavily on her cane, her heart beating rapidly.

Alan looked up Nick Grainger's profile and found he had no record, not even a parking ticket, which was rare in Boston. It listed his address in the Quincy area which might mean he had money because it was one of the wealthy communities.

Searching Google for a description of the location, Alan saw that it was an old building that probably had a lot of charm. He was surprised to see available rentals for under $2400 but guessed it would be for a small studio. Alan thought that young professionals just starting out would jump at the chance to live there. Quincy also had a strong political contingent, and it could be that Grainger had political aspirations. This gave Alan another thought. He called Sidney.

"Well, my friend," Sidney said, "I haven't heard how you're doing with this weather. Are you at work?"

"Yeah... storms don't stop crimes from happening, unfortunately. You in town too?"

"No, I took some work home. I'd rather be cooped up here than in the city."

Alan knew Sidney's apartment was as sophisticated as his friend, with one of the best views of the Charles River. "I'm sure you're not suffering much. I need to ask your opinion... if someone works for the city council in any capacity, is that a step to other political appointments?"

Sidney hesitated. "I suppose you're not going to tell me what this is about... "

"Not yet. I'm working on a long shot... "

"Okay... I would say yes. Especially if this person has a background in political science which would indicate a desire to get involved. But there are lots of other ways too."

Alan gave this some thought. "Let's say he has a voice in the community. My guess is that he has a high degree of control over many aspects of the community. Because of this, I expect that any advancement, even a small one, would be a step forward. One more observation... if this person lived in a wealthy suburb like Quincy, would there be more opportunity for advancement in politics?"

Sidney let out a long laugh. "You can live anywhere near this city and get involved in politics! This is where it happens!"

Both men laughed. You couldn't deny that Boston and politics were sleeping together. Thanking his friend for the candid conversation, Alan looked outside to see the thick flakes of snow falling. He had to get home.

THURSDAY, FEBRUARY 13TH

Alan was worried when he didn't hear from Sylvia. He had already been in his office for two hours and usually had a phone call from her by now. He didn't like to jump to conclusions, but something wasn't right. He had a nagging feeling that someone found out her identity. He decided to go to the shelter and talk with Deacon Martin.

Just as he was reaching for his heavy overcoat, Enrique walked in shaking the snow off his boots. "Where are you going? It's freezing out there!"

"I haven't heard from Sylvia. Do you want to come with me?"

Enrique nodded. "Let me get some coffee first."

Both men braced themselves against the cold as they walked quickly to an unmarked car. The reliable engine started quickly with a blast of heat coming from the fans. "Let's start at the shelter and then go to the station," Alan said.

People were lined up outside the shelter, huddled together to keep warm. The doors were closed which surprised the officers as they pulled up in front. "Shouldn't it be open by now?" Enrique wondered.

"Let's go find out." Alan knocked on the glass door and saw Levi quickly walk over to let them inside. "Why are you closed?"

"We're short-staffed again. We had to get things organized with only a few volunteers. But I'm opening now." The cold air rushed into the room along with a long line of people seeking warmth and some food. "I've got to help out... are you here for someone?"

Alan nodded. "Have you seen Trevor Reynolds?"

"Not since yesterday. He might be at the station."

"Do you know if he was talking with an older woman who had a cane? She was homeless appearing... "

"I saw her here last night for dinner. I think Trevor may know her because they were talking the other day."

Alan was impressed with Levi and how he kept an eye out for the people he served. "I'll let you get back to work."

Looking through the crowd and not seeing Sylvia, the two men decided to check the station. Alan knew it was useless to try to phone her because of the danger he might put her in. They had agreed she would phone him only in an emergency.

The station was filled with commuters either coming to work or trying to get back home to beat the storm. Bostonians knew how to deal with the weather and still get things done. Working from home was always an option, even when you had to rush in and pick up what you needed. Looking around for Sylvia, Alan noticed a cane lying on the floor by the stairs. He went over to pick it up when he saw Trevor standing three feet away.

"Trevor Reynolds? Did you spend the night here?" Alan asked.

Trevor stayed mute.

"I'm looking for someone. Do you know who owns

this cane?"

Trevor's eyebrows raised and he stared at Alan and then shook his head.

"We understand you were speaking with an older lady at the shelter last night. We're looking for her... we need to question her about the murder." Alan wanted to change the narrative so that Trevor would think Sylvia was a suspect. "What do you know about her?"

Trevor was confused. He thought the lady was an informant, but maybe he had it all wrong. If that was the case, he still didn't know where she went after she left the station last night. "She left here around ten last night. Beat's me where she went." He walked quickly away.

Alan tried Sylvia's hotel room number. No answer. Enrique approached him with his head shaking. "I can't find her. Any ideas?"

Alan picked up the fallen cane and thought for a minute. "She was at the shelter, then here. Someone might have suspected her... these are the only two places she was seen. Now I'm thinking we better call the hospitals."

Dr. Meyers was still on duty when Alan called Mass General. She looked up the recent intakes and told him there was a woman who was found lying on the ground near the station last night.

"Was she homeless?" Alan asked.

"She didn't have any ID on her, but she looked desperate. We gave her something to sleep through the night and I believe she's awake now. What should I do?"

Alan asked to connect him to the room.

Sylvia was groggy when the phone rang, but she answered anyway. "Hello, who is this?"

Alan was relieved to hear the familiar voice. "Sylvia, it's Alan. How are you?"

"I guess I'm okay. Do you know what happened?"

Alan told her he would be at the hospital in ten minutes.

The streets were icy and barely manageable. Alan told Enrique to drop him at the hospital entrance and then return to the precinct. He would get a ride back later.

When he entered Sylvia's room he was immediately worried about his friend. She had bruises on her face and her arm was in a cast. "What do you remember?"

Sylvia grimaced slightly as she attempted to sit up. "I was at the shelter when the guy called Cal came running in saying that the police had Vince Robarts in custody. He yelled at everyone to be careful because the police were watching everything they did. So, I left and went to the station."

"Did someone follow you?"

"I wish I paid more attention, but the weather was so cold, and I walked quickly. I found a place to sit at the station and then Trevor Reynolds found me and started harassing me. He must have followed me there now that I think about it. At that point I decided to go back to the hotel."

Alan interrupted her, "Did you drop your cane?"

"I put it down so I could call you. I was standing in a corner out of sight of everyone, trying to be discreet and then that's all I remember."

"Do you still have your phone?"

"You can check... my things are in that drawer."

Alan searched through the drawer and found nothing. "Okay... so someone has the phone. We don't have a GPS on it... it's a burner... but maybe we'll locate it once we find out who did this to you. Do you have any idea?"

"Well, first I would say Cal... the guy who was yelling. He knew I was talking with Vince the other day."

"What about Trevor?"

"No... I would doubt it. His role is more of a caretaker. But he might know who to talk to."

"I'm going to have an officer outside your room. Do you want me to notify your family?"

"I'd like to get out of here and go home, Alan. Now that my identity's blown, I think I'm done here. Hopefully they'll discharge me later today or early tomorrow."

"We can have someone drive you to the hotel to get your things. Can you call someone to drive you back to Albany?"

"Don't worry about me... I've got friends who will drop everything. Sorry I couldn't help more."

Alan reassured her that they were now closer to finding the killer because of her. In fact, it was her spotting Ethan West that helped get him arrested. Alan thanked her and promised to keep her posted on the case.

Now he had to find out who attacked Sylvia.

FRIDAY, FEBRUARY 14TH

Alan had a restless night. He had stayed up late trying to piece together what Sylvia had reported and how this might have a connection to the homeless population. He called Officer Lane before he had his first cup of coffee.

Sasha was at the precinct trying to decide when to brave the weather and go out on patrol. Connie was sitting next to her, sipping coffee, and wishing they could just go home. When Sasha's phone rang, they both hoped it wasn't an order. But it was.

"Yes, sir. Officer Beale and I are both available. We'll leave now."

"We're going to the station to look for cameras and talk to people." She filled Connie in on what happened to Sylvia. Both officers had been unaware that an undercover agent was involved and would have to be cautious. It sounded like people were suspicious and upset by police involvement and might overreact to their presence. Checking their equipment, they bundled up and hurried out the door.

Nick Grainger was distraught. He began working through all the possible scenarios to make sure his name wouldn't be linked to any trail of evidence. He hoped his gaming activities wouldn't make him culpable because online researchers always wanted to link increased aggression to gamers. Now that the police knew he was involved with those types of games, he might be a suspect.

Ethan West was an idiot! He should have vetted him! Nick was angry at himself for not paying closer attention to that psychopath and his excitement about killing people in the games. All the talk he spouted about 'kills' while gaming was probably some sort of reality for him. Nick knew it was the accumulation of risk factors, like the ongoing criminal activities he should have found out about the guy, that might have led him to violence.

Another thought came to Nick... did that put him in jeopardy for killing the cop? He knew it sounded unreasonable, but some things could be traced back to him. He had sent a volunteer out to follow the cop that was killed that day and try to explain what the organization was all about. Did that person kill him? Nick picked up his phone and called Levi.

The shelter was busy. Keeping up with the flow of people was almost impossible, and when Levi's phone rang, he tried to ignore it. But it rang again. "Yeah... " he answered curtly.

"Levi, it's Nick. Do you see Cal there?"

Levi looked around. "Yeah... he's here."

"I need to talk to him."

When Cal came to the phone, Nick spoke quickly. "We need to talk. Get over here." Then he hung up. Cal had been homeless for years and was well-known at the shelter, helping Levi with custodial jobs. But he worked for Nick, too. He oversaw problems that might impact the volunteer organization and kept Nick informed of eruptions in the camps like stealing or fighting. In fact, it was Cal who reported the illnesses to Nick, and even suspected it to be more than a virus. But he didn't want to speculate. Staying uninvolved and out of sight was more important to Cal.

When Connie and Sasha arrived at the station, they were amazed by how many people occupied the benches and the floors and were leaning up against the walls. It had become the only shelter in the city, even for people who couldn't get back home because of the snow. Looking around for surveillance cameras, they spotted three that pointed in different directions. Once they found the security guard, they were escorted to a room to view the tapes. Reluctant to admit what they were searching for, the officers decided to get copies of the last three nights and return to the precinct.

Enrique was becoming more convinced that Nick Grainger was involved with the murder. He decided to go meet with him again and ask more questions. What was he doing at the time of the murder? Who was he protecting besides Ethan West?

Enrique knew that not many businesses were open due to the freezing weather, but when he arrived at the volunteer building, he saw a light shining in Grainger's office. Just as he was getting out of his car, he saw a sketchy looking big guy enter the building. Following the man cautiously, Enrique watched him walk into Nick Grainger's office. From the hallway, Enrique stopped and listened as shouting began.

"Did you kill that cop?" Grainger sounded furious.

"No! Why would I?" Cal sounded heated.

"I asked you to follow him and talk with him. He had a

grudge against street people, and I thought you might clear things up. Did you talk with him?"

"No! He stopped to talk with another cop, and I just kept going. And then he got killed! I had nothing to do with it!"

Enrique listened and knew this might be true. Wagner had spoken to Officer Erickson that day on his way to the subway. If it wasn't Grainger and it wasn't Cal... who followed Wagner and killed him? Enrique slipped away and called Alan.

"This is getting to be a mess!" Alan said. He was driving back from Peabody where he left Sylvia at the hotel. "It looks like we don't have a suspect yet. Let's bring in Cal and Grainger. I need to talk with them."

Enrique called for backup and waited.

Alan could hear a loud voice when he walked into the precinct. Nick Grainger was holding court, demanding to have his lawyer contacted. He wasn't in an interview room but was pacing back and forth in the squad room, waiting for the Detective to arrive. When he noticed Alan, he stopped pacing and glared.

"Mr. Grainger, I'm sorry to keep you waiting. It's the weather... you know... please follow me to my office." Grainger looked appeased and complied.

Alan had no reason to suspect Nick, but he needed to clear some things up. "Mr. Grainger, I have a few questions to ask you about your conversation with Officer Wagner on the day he was killed. You said he wanted to apply to be a volunteer. Didn't you already have his application?"

"He had filled out an online form which is only an introduction. I showed you that when you were at my office.

He had the idea that this was all he needed." Nick leaned back in his chair, seeming more relaxed.

"Did he understand that there was more information needed?"

Nick looked up at the ceiling, trying to remember how the conversation went. "He seemed frustrated by the delay. I told him about going through training and he argued that being a police officer was enough to waylay that part. I explained that it was required."

Alan wanted to remind Nick about letting Ethan West slide through the system but decided to move on. "When he left your office, what was his mood?"

"Well, he appeared to want to think about volunteering with us. My thought was that he might try someplace else."

"Did you follow him?"

"No."

"What time did you leave your office that day?"

Nick stared blankly. "I'm not sure. Are you accusing me of something?"

Alan shook his head. "We're only trying to find out why someone would target our officer. Let me ask you this... Did you send someone to follow him?"

Nick looked uncomfortable. "Did Cal say this?" He knew they had him in custody.

"Yes. Why did you send him?"

Letting out a deep breath, Nick tried to explain. "Sometimes people need to hear from someone who is homeless about how we help. My organization has reached out to thousands of people who struggle, and we always want to set the record straight. Your officer seemed to have, let's say, a curious attitude about what we do."

"That's an interesting thought... why curious?"

"Detective, we work with a wide variety of people who have distinct needs and challenges. We prefer volunteers who are patient and compassionate. I didn't get the impression that your officer understood that he needed to take a moment and consider what skills he had to offer. Our training program is designed to match people to their skill levels."

Alan thought about Wagner's attitude that day when he argued with Officer Erickson. He decided to take another approach. "I understand you have personal contacts all over the city who help keep your organization in line. In fact, how do you keep track of your volunteers?"

Nick nodded and smirked. "That's a great question. For instance, Levi Martin at the shelter is one of my contacts. If anything happens that I should know about he calls me. And I reach out to him if I'm worried about a volunteer."

"Do you have any idea who killed Officer Wagner?" Alan stared intently at Grainger, hoping to catch him off guard.

"No, I do not." Nick looked sincere. If he was playing politics, Alan thought, it was working. "May I go?"

Alan hesitated. What more could he ask of Grainger? He had no proof he was involved, except for having spoken to Wagner minutes before he was killed. "How do you know Cal? Does he work for you?"

Nick sighed. "Yes, he does. I need someone who can easily roam throughout the camps and contact me if there's a problem or something we should be aware of. He's been with me for over a year."

Alan nodded. "Who else do you employ besides Levi Martin and Cal?"

"Besides my volunteers, just staff people, some who are

temps. We have an accountant and secretary."

"How did you first meet Ethan West?"

Now Nick was in trouble. Looking down at his hands while trying to decide what to say, Enrique entered the office. "Do you have a minute?"

Alan looked at Nick and said, "Please stay here. I want to continue our conversation."

Enrique told Alan that Cal wanted to talk to the lead detective.

Cal had been waiting in an interview room for over an hour. He was a big guy and seemed to overload the chair he was sitting at. He had placed his knit cap on the table and was drumming his fingers next to it.

Alan and Enrique both entered the room. Alan took out his notebook and began. "Can we have your last name?"

"Ross."

Enrique handed Alan a report that listed information about Cal's history. "We see you're from Jersey. How long have you been in Boston?"

"About two years."

"How long have you been homeless?"

"Same."

"So, it says here that you are a mechanic. Are you looking for work?"

"Yeah."

"Where were you around 5:00, Friday, January 24th, when Officer Wagner was killed in the subway tunnel?"

"On the way to my camp."

"How can you verify the exact time?"

"Because I was supposed to talk to that officer... the one who was killed... but when I saw him stop and argue with another guy, I just kept going. It was starting to snow, and I had to get back to my camp and start my fire."

"Did you see anyone else following the policeman?"

"No. But I did talk to one of Grainger's volunteers. He was on his way to the subway and wanted to know what I was doing. He's into control... always sneaking around and asking questions. We all stay away from him."

"What's his name?"

"West... Ethan."

Alan and Enrique looked at each other. That made Ethan West in the vicinity of the crime.

They brought West back in to question him. Because he had spent some time in jail, he looked worn out, but the Detectives saw immediately that his attitude was showing. He glared at them and demanded a lawyer.

Alan raised his eyebrows and nodded slightly. "We'll be glad to get you one. But, as you know, with this kind of weather, you'll probably have to wait a day or two. Maybe you can answer a few questions for us in the meantime."

Ethan remained silent.

"Do you know Cal Ross?"

No response.

"He tells us he saw you walking to the subway on the evening that Officer Wagner was killed. Do you recall this?"

No response.

"The thing is, if we have you at the scene of the crime, we'll need a statement from you." Alan changed his tactic. "Maybe you saw something that will help us locate the killer."

Ethan looked uncomfortable but remained silent.

Alan brought out a folder and opened it. "Mr. West,

you've got quite a record. It looks like you have been suspected of stealing, bribery, larceny... and now poisoning. I guess we could assume you have little concern for the law."

Ethan glared. He was getting angry.

"We know that psychopaths need control. If someone gets in their way, they react aggressively. We also know that some very violent video games were found at your apartment along with a list of complaints you have against certain people. One of the complaints was getting even with the police. We'll go back to your apartment, now, and search for evidence. What will we find?"

Ethan slammed his fists on the table. "I want a lawyer!"

Connie and Sasha were busy reviewing the surveillance tapes when they saw Cal Ross walk through the station. Noting his ragged clothes, they suspected he was homeless and was being questioned, although they didn't know why. When they saw Nick Grainger being led into Detective Sharp's office, their curiosity was sparked even more. Maybe both men had something to do with the assault on the woman in the hospital.

An hour later, Connie stopped the tapes she was viewing. "Hey... Sasha, come here a minute. I think I found something." She was staring at the same man who just walked through the station... the homeless guy. "He looks suspicious... watch him look around a couple times as if someone might see him. This is the vicinity where Sylvia was found."

Sasha watched the scene with interest. "Let's get this to Detective Sharp now. I think the guy's still here."

Alan heard the knock on the interview room door and

went to answer. "Important?" he asked quickly.

Sasha whispered when Alan walked over to the door. "The guy you're with... we have him on tape around the area where your friend says she was accosted."

Alan nodded. "Bring me some photos."

Sasha hurried back to get copies of the film.

Alan motioned to Enrique, and they walked out of the interview room. "We've now got three suspects. Cal Ross, Nick Grainger, and Ethan West. All three belong to the same group which leads me to believe that one of them killed Officer Wagner. But we need motive. We know that Ethan West was using poison to kill people, but why or how were the other two involved?"

Enrique nodded. "Let's keep them in custody a while longer. I'll contact Agent Lee and meet you in the conference room."

Agent Lee was watching the heavy snow falling outside the window when Enrique approached him. "Do you have time to meet?"

Lee smiled, as if relieved not to have to endure the cold weather. "Certainly. Let me get my notes."

The three men grabbed coffee before sitting down at the old table in the conference room. In front of the room was the white board they had used before with all the previous information detailed on it. Alan brought Lee up to date on the last 24-hour events and who they had in custody now. "Any ideas?"

Lee flipped through his notes until he found something and then walked over to the board. "Ethan West is a psychopath. We know this. He easily manipulates and controls people who he considers far below him. This would be Cal Ross. What do you know about Mr. Ross?"

Alan opened a file he had received earlier. "He's 37, from Jersey, worked as a mechanic and has been in Boston for two years. We're waiting for a full police record on him. It should come in any minute... things are slow due to the weather."

Lee nodded. "If he's telling the truth, what motive would either Ethan West or Cal Ross have for killing an officer? Did they know him? This seems to be the question nobody has answered. Why Officer Wagner?"

Alan stood up and approached Lee. "You're right. Why?"

Lee looked at the board. "Let's go back a minute. What were the two officers arguing about on the street?"

Alan tried to recall what Officer Erickson had told him. "It was about Wagner's attitude on the homeless. They had argued at the station and Erickson wanted to clear some things up."

Lee nodded. "I've attempted to contact him... left messages. But he's not returned my calls. Tell me about this officer... would he have any reason to attack Officer Wagner?"

Alan filled Lee in on the problems Erickson had earlier in his career. "He told me he meets with a sponsor regularly to keep his aggressive tendencies in check. His arguments with Wagner were defensive... he thought Wagner was too opinionated and unable to compromise. At least that's what I picked up when I spoke with him."

Alan looked at Enrique. "What's his schedule?"

Enrique picked up his phone and searched the precinct schedule on his app. "He should be here now. Let me go see if he's available."

Three minutes later Enrique returned with an alarmed look on his face. "Erickson's been on personal leave for over a week. I called HR and he hasn't notified them of when he'll be returning."

"Did you get his address?" Alan had an uncomfortable feeling. Enrique nodded and went to get his coat.

Officer Erickson lived in Woburn, a city twenty-five minutes from Boston. With the streets being cleared of snow, the drive was faster than earlier in the day. The Detectives remained silent, hoping they were wrong about Erickson. When they arrived at his house, the lights were on in the windows, and so the men walked up the path and knocked.

Erickson opened the door. "I've been expecting you."

Erickson looked years older than he had weeks before. He hadn't slept for days, maybe longer. His unshaven beard and dirty hair were a dark shade of grey, and his eyes were red rimmed and appeared blank, as if resigned to his fate. He was wearing a dark blue sweatsuit that hung on him, and his feet were bare. This was a man in distress.

He led them into a living room that was piled with food containers, empty water bottles, and discarded wrappers. Beer and liquor bottles were tossed on the floor. Quietly, he murmured, "I know... it looks like a cliché... wallowing in pity. I just wanted to give up."

The detectives remained standing, even as Erickson flopped onto the sofa, throwing some containers onto the floor. "Are you going to read me my rights?"

Alan shook his head. "We're going to take you to the precinct and talk. Can you get yourself ready?"

Erickson stared and seemed in a daze. Enrique moved to help him, but Erickson shoved him aside and stood up. "I can do this." They watched him walk slowly into another room. Alan nodded to Enrique to follow him.

It's a sad day when a police officer is accused of a crime. And even worse when he is accused of killing another officer. By the time Erickson had been interviewed and given a signed statement, the precinct was buzzing with anxiety. A failure to act responsibly was one thing, but to harm another officer was beyond the rules of police conduct.

Lee, Alan, and Enrique sat in the conference room at the end of the day in silence. The two cases, in some dreadful way, had ended with a marked sense of tragedy. Homeless people were poisoned, as if they didn't have enough worries in their lives, and Officer Wagner's life had been cut short. According to Erickson, he just snapped. All his training and behavioral support did not compel or remind him to step back and de-escalate the confrontation. Erickson, himself, was only a paycheck away from being homeless. He had lost money playing online poker and didn't have the means to recover. Wagner's insistence on deriding anyone who was homeless had riled him. And when he approached the younger officer to try to explain, he was met with more obnoxious words casting the blame on to street people. Erickson had reminded Wagner how desperate people might be, even desperate enough to find hiding places in the tunnels of the subway. That was when Wagner started towards the tunnel. Erickson apparently lost control and followed Wagner. He yelled to him to stop, and when Wagner turned around Erickson attacked him. It was not a calculated response, just a gut reaction that wasn't meant to kill. Erickson had panicked and reached for a cord in his pocket that he kept for tying up evidence bags. At the point of strangling Officer Wagner, Erickson knew it was his last moment as a free man.

SATURDAY, FEBRUARY 15TH

Agent Lee stood at the door of Alan's office. "May I come in?"

Alan had been lost in thought and busy writing his report when he looked up and smiled warmly at the agent. "Please come in. I thought you might be gone by now. The weather's better today."

Lee walked in and took a chair beside Alan's desk. "I have enjoyed working with you, Detective. I believe I've learned much these past few days."

Alan looked surprised. "I can't imagine that anything we do here is something new for you. We've appreciated how you kept us on track and helped solve both cases. I'm impressed with your techniques and analytical skills."

Lee bowed his head slightly. "You have led the way, Detective. I admire your humanistic approach, emphasizing that people are innately good. I imagine you see a lot of adversaries each day and sometimes it must take a good deal of strength to see the brighter side of humanity."

Alan thought for a minute. "My strength comes from

the good people I work with. I believe we're doing the best we can to protect and serve. Thank you for your help, Lee, I think you have a very bright future."

Lee stood up and bowed slightly to Alan. "Until we meet again."

Made in the USA
Columbia, SC
30 May 2024